Seventh Chapter

by

Kathi Daley

I want to thank the very talented Jessica Fischer for the cover art.

I so appreciate Bruce Curran, who is always ready and willing to answer my cyber questions; Jayme Maness for helping out with the book clubs; and Peggy Hyndman for helping sleuth out those pesky typos.

And, of course, thanks to the readers and bloggers in my life, who make doing what I do possible.

Thank you to Randy Ladenheim-Gil for the editing.

And finally, I want to thank my husband Ken for allowing me time to write by taking care of everything else.

Books by Kathi Daley

Come for the murder, stay for the romance.

Zoe Donovan Cozy Mystery:

Halloween Hijinks
The Trouble With Turkeys
Christmas Crazy
Cupid's Curse
Big Bunny Bump-off
Beach Blanket Barbie
Maui Madness
Derby Divas
Haunted Hamlet
Turkeys, Tuxes, and Tabbies
Christmas Cozy
Alaskan Alliance
Matrimony Meltdown
Soul Surrender
Heavenly Honeymoon
Hopscotch Homicide
Ghostly Graveyard
Santa Sleuth
Shamrock Shenanigans
Kitten Kaboodle
Costume Catastrophe
Candy Cane Caper
Holiday Hangover
Easter Escapade
Camp Carter
Trick or Treason
Reindeer Roundup
Hippity Hoppity Homicide

Firework Fiasco
Henderson House – *August 2018*

Zimmerman Academy The New Normal
Ashton Falls Cozy Cookbook

Tj Jensen Paradise Lake Mysteries by Henery Press:

Pumpkins in Paradise
Snowmen in Paradise
Bikinis in Paradise
Christmas in Paradise
Puppies in Paradise
Halloween in Paradise
Treasure in Paradise
Fireworks in Paradise
Beaches in Paradise

Whales and Tails Cozy Mystery:

Romeow and Juliet
The Mad Catter
Grimm's Furry Tail
Much Ado About Felines
Legend of Tabby Hollow
Cat of Christmas Past
A Tale of Two Tabbies
The Great Catsby
Count Catula
The Cat of Christmas Present
A Winter's Tail
The Taming of the Tabby
Frankencat

The Cat of Christmas Future
Farewell to Felines
A Whisker in Time – *September 2018*
The Catsgiving Feast – *November 2018*

Writers' Retreat Southern Seashore Mystery:

First Case
Second Look
Third Strike
Fourth Victim
Fifth Night
Sixth Cabin
Seventh Chapter

Rescue Alaska Paranormal Mystery:

Finding Justice
Finding Answers
Finding Courage - *September 2018*
Finding Christmas – *November 2018*

A Tess and Tilly Mystery:

The Christmas Letter
The Valentine Mystery
The Mother's Day Mishap
The Halloween House
The Thanksgiving Trip – *November 2018*

Haunting by the Sea:
Homecoming by the Sea
Secrets by the Sea
Missing by the Sea – *October 2018*

Sand and Sea Hawaiian Mystery:
Murder at Dolphin Bay
Murder at Sunrise Beach
Murder at the Witching Hour
Murder at Christmas
Murder at Turtle Cove
Murder at Water's Edge
Murder at Midnight

Seacliff High Mystery:
The Secret
The Curse
The Relic
The Conspiracy
The Grudge
The Shadow
The Haunting

Road to Christmas Romance:
Road to Christmas Past

The Writers' Retreat Residents

Jillian (Jill) Hanford

Jillian is a newspaper reporter who moved to Gull Island after her much-older brother, Garrett Hanford, had a stroke and was no longer able to run the resort he'd inherited.

Jackson (Jack) Jones

Jack is a nationally acclaimed author of hard-core mysteries and thrillers. Despite his success as a novelist, he'd always dreamed of writing for a newspaper, so he gave up his penthouse apartment and bought the failing *Gull Island News*.

George Baxter

George is a writer of traditional whodunit mysteries. He'd been a friend of Garrett Hanford's since they were boys and spent many winters at the resort penning his novels.

Clara Kline

Clara is a self-proclaimed psychic who writes fantasy and paranormal mysteries. Clara decided to move to the retreat after she had a vision that she would find her soul mate living within its walls.

Alex Cole

Alex is a fun and flirty millennial who made his first million writing science fiction when he was just twenty-two.

Brit Baxter

Brit is George Baxter's niece. Her real strength is in social networking and understanding the dynamics behind the information individuals choose to share on the internet.

Victoria Vance

Victoria is a romance author who lives the life she writes about in her steamy novels.

Garrett Hanford

Garrett isn't a writer, but he owns the resort and is becoming one of the gang. He had a stroke that ended his ability to run the resort as a family vacation spot. He has lived on Gull Island his entire life and has a lot to offer the Mystery Mastermind Group.

Townsfolk

Deputy Rick Savage

Rick is not only the island's main source of law enforcement, he's a volunteer force unto himself.

Mayor Betty Sue Bell

Betty Sue is a homegrown Southern lady who owns a beauty parlor called Betty Boop's Beauty Salon.

Gertie Newsome

Gertie is the owner of Gertie's on the Wharf. Southern born and bred, she believes in the magic of the South and the passion of its people. She shares her home with a ghost named Mortie, who has been a regular part of her life for over thirty years.

Meg Collins

Meg is a volunteer at the island museum and the organizer of the turtle rescue squad.

Brooke Johnson

Brooke is a teacher and mother who works hard in her spare time as volunteer coordinator for the community.

The Cast

Victim:
Bosley Newman

Candidates for Island Council
Brenda Tamari—teacher
William Quarterly—owns Gull Island Hardware
Jeffrey Riverton—owns both the Riverton Hotel and
the Riverton Coastal Resort
Glen Pierson—endorsed by the Castle Foundation

Founding Sons:
Sam Castle
Ron Remand
Zane Carson
Billy Waller

Fishermen living in the area who are on the witness
list:
Trout Kellerman
Buck Johnston
Tizzy Tizdale

Others:
Vincent O'Brian—used to be in business with Billy;
dined with him prior to his death
Logan Franklin—works at the marina; rented Bosley
a boat
Oswald Bollinger—scientist involved in the area a
century ago
Bianca Castle—Sam's ex
Jessica Carson—Zane's sister
Viv Castle—Sam's sister

Chapter 1

Monday, October 22

"As most of you are aware, we have four candidates competing for two open seats on the island council," Mayor Betty Sue Bell announced to a packed auditorium. "The purpose of the meeting tonight is to give everyone who's interested a chance to meet the candidates and to ask any questions you may have before heading to the polls next month. Those of you who had questions were asked to submit them to one of the monitors prior to the start of the meeting. The questions have been grouped and categorized, and we'll ask as many as we have time for. Each question selected will be asked to all four candidates. Before I begin, are there any questions regarding the procedure I've just outlined?"

I angled myself toward the front of the room so I could capture the photographs I'd come to take for the *Gull Island News*. My boyfriend and newspaper owner Jack Jones had intended to attend the meeting but had gotten held up interviewing witnesses to a house fire. The third house fire in the past three weeks. I was sure there was a story there and so was he.

"I'm going to begin by introducing each of the candidates," Betty Sue continued after she'd answered a few questions from those who hadn't been completely clear on what to expect from the meeting. "Our first candidate, Brenda Tamari, is sitting to my far left." Everyone in the room, including me, glanced toward the petite forty-five-year-old with short blond hair and a sunny smile. "Brenda teaches mathematics at the high school and has been a resident of Gull Island for almost twelve years. When she isn't busy at the high school either teaching or coaching, she volunteers at the local youth center, where she oversees both the girls soccer team and the girls basketball team. Brenda has been endorsed by the local teachers association as well as the community youth athletic league."

I took a photo of Brenda while Betty Sue caught her breath. She really was in her element. When I'd first moved to the island and was told that the vivacious woman who seemed to have mastered the ability to talk a mile a minute was also the mayor, I'd been skeptical, but after having a chance to get to know her, I can see she's perfect for the job.

After a few seconds, Betty Sue continued. "Our second candidate, William Quarterly, is sitting directly to my left." I glanced at the tall, dark-haired man who looked to be in his late thirties. "William owns Gull Island Hardware and is an active member of both the merchants association and the Gull Island Chamber of Commerce. He's been endorsed by both. William has lived on Gull Island for eight years. During that time…"

I glanced away as Betty Sue continued to list William's accomplishments. When she wasn't actively performing her duties as mayor, she owned and operated Betty Boop's, a hair salon where the stylists dressed like women from the fifties and sixties. Tonight, however, Betty Sue wore a black dress suit and sensible pumps. Her makeup was toned down, her hair styled to reflect sophistication rather than sass.

"Hey, Jill," Meg Collins, the director and head volunteer of both the local museum and the turtle rescue squad, whispered after she sidled up to me. "Is George here?"

"I haven't seen him," I whispered back. Meg and George Baxter, one of the writers who lived at the retreat I helped to run, were dating. "He's presenting a project to the Mastermind group later this evening, so he might be getting ready for that. I mentioned to him that I was attending this meeting, and he said he was familiar with all the candidates and already knew who he planned to vote for, so he thought he might skip it."

"I'm not surprised. George is very decisive, and I knew he'd done his homework on all the candidates." Meg glanced at the woman who was waiting patiently to her left. "Jill Hanford, this is Lisa Dalton. Jill runs the writers' retreat where George lives. Lisa is a new member of the turtle rescue squad."

"Happy to meet you, Lisa." I smiled in greeting just as Mayor Bell moved on to the third candidate.

"Nice to meet you too," Lisa answered. "Meg has told me a lot about you and the group at the resort."

I smiled at her but didn't say more as Betty Sue continued. "The man sitting to my far right is our third candidate. For those of you who might not know him, his name is Jeffrey Riverton. Mr. Riverton owns both the Riverton Hotel and the Riverton Coastal Resort. He's lived on Gull Island for five years and is being endorsed by both the lodging association and the visitors bureau."

I knew Riverton, a tall, thin man with graying hair and sharp features, the least of the four candidates. His properties were nice and attracted an affluent clientele, but I'd heard rumors that the reason he wanted to be voted on to the council was so he could push through a project that many felt was much too large for our little island. The project had been presented to the current council twice and had been met with resistance by the majority of the council members.

"And finally," Betty Sue continued, glancing to the handsome, dark-haired man sitting closest to her, "the gentleman directly to my right is Glen Pierson. Glen is a real estate executive and a member of the local historical society. He's lived on Gull Island for the past six years and plans to work to ensure the integrity of the community as it was originally envisioned. Glen has been endorsed by both the historical society and the Castle Foundation."

There was a level of murmuring throughout the crowd. I had the feeling Glen Pierson and Jeffrey Riverton were going to go head to head on more than one occasion before this election was over. Riverton seemed to be all about development, while Pierson, who was being backed by the Castle Foundation, was all about preserving the integrity of what currently existed. The Foundation was run by Sam Castle's ex-wife, Bianca.

"It looks as if we're going to have an interesting race," Meg commented.

"It does seem as if there's a lot of energy being generated by all four candidates."

"Being a member of the council is sort of a big thing around these parts, so there's usually a good pool of candidates," Meg added.

The town council had eight members. Four of the seats were honorary, held by a descendant of each of the four of the island's founding fathers. Traditionally, the seat had been handed down from eldest son to eldest son, so the seats, as well as the men who held them, were referred to as the founding sons. Currently, those seats were occupied by Sam Castle, Billy Waller, Zane Carson, and Ron Remand. The other four seats were elected positions. Each elected council member served a four-year term. The terms were staggered, so two seats came up for election every two years.

Betty Sue glanced around the room. "Before we begin with the questions prepared for our candidates, let's give them all a round of appreciation for the work they already do in our community."

I took several more photos while everyone applauded.

"I imagine George must be planning to ask the Mastermind group for help regarding Bosley Newman's disappearance," Meg said while we waited for the noise to die down.

"I believe that's his plan. I'm sure the group will want to help out, given that Bosley is a fellow writer, although he's only been missing since Saturday. Brit seems to think he's absentminded and often forgets to check in on a somewhat regular basis."

"Brit said the same thing to me," Meg admitted, referring to George's niece, another member of the Mastermind group. "But George is really worried, and I trust his instincts. I planned to attend the meeting this evening, if you don't think the others will mind. I've worked with Bosley during the past couple of weeks, and I believe I have some insight into where he was going with his research."

I waved at a woman I knew who'd just entered the room through the side door. "I don't think anyone will mind if you join us. We aren't meeting until eight and are skipping dinner tonight because I had this meeting to attend. I have to leave here at seven thirty, though, whether the meeting is over or not. Hopefully, Jack will be back from the fire he went to cover by then as well."

"I'll plan to come, then," Meg said as Betty Sue prepared to ask the candidates the first of what I was sure were many questions. "I think I'm going to scoot out now to grab a bite to eat. I'll see you at eight."

I glanced at Lisa. "It was nice to meet you."

"You too. I just moved to the island, but I want get involved, so I'm sure I'll see you around."

I returned my attention to the front of the room, where the candidates took turns answering questions. All four seemed intelligent and committed to their causes. I assumed any of them would be a good choice for the two open seats. While it was my job to present the facts and then allow those who read the newspaper article to make up their own minds, personally, I'd like to see Brenda end up with one of the seats. At present, the council consisted of eight males, and I thought a female perspective would help to add balance. I'd only lived on the island for a little over a year, and the council seats only came open on even-numbered years, so this was the first election I'd been present to observe, but from what I'd heard from others who'd been around for a while, the island council was stacked by older men who wielded their power with iron fists.

"Hey there, pretty lady."

"Hey, Sully," I responded to the local bar owner and all-around flirt. "I'm surprised to see you here. You don't seem like the political sort."

"Normally I'm not, but Jeffrey Riverton has been making some noise about buying up a bunch of properties on Main Street, and I'd hate to see that happen. Our little piece of heaven is quaint. It's the independent business owner who's going to keep it that way. Glen Pierson understands that. I think Quarterly does as well."

"What about Brenda Tamari?"

Sully shrugged. "I figure she doesn't really have a shot at one of the seats, so my efforts are better served backing Pierson and Quarterly."

I frowned. "Why don't you think Brenda has a shot? Is it because she's a woman?"

"It's exactly because she's a woman. The island council has historically been a group of powerful men. I realize that idea might be a bit antiquated, but I don't see it changing anytime soon. You're new to the island, so you may not realize that the folks in these parts want to adhere to tradition, and right or wrong, our tradition is that the council is a meeting of men."

I rolled my eyes. When I'd moved from New York to Gull Island, I knew I was going to have to learn to deal with a slower pace and a more conservative culture, but I hadn't known the move was going to transport me back to the fifties.

******

By the time I was able to sneak out of the meeting and return to the resort, where I lived with my half brother, Garrett, and ten other writers, Jack had arrived. We quickly caught up on our evenings while we wolfed down sandwiches. Usually, I took the time to prepare a meal, but we didn't want to be late joining the others in the living room. When I'd walked through, I'd seen George had already set chairs around the fireplace, and several of the writers had already gathered to chat.

"Three house fires in three weeks is really concerning me," I said as I dug into my tuna on toast.

"It does seem like a pattern is emerging. Not only does it look like all three fires were intentionally set but they're similar in terms of size and location as well."

"I can't believe we're dealing with another arsonist after what happened last year."

Jack shrugged. "I guess arson is fairly common. All we can do right now is wait and see how it all turns out. How did the question-and-answer session go?"

He agreed with my opinion that it would be nice to have a female presence on the council, and also understood the importance of tradition and those who would fight to keep it. I made a comment about a tight race having the potential to create friction, and Jack said the campaign would most likely get nasty in the final weeks before the election in November. To this point, both Brenda and William had played nice, but Riverton had been campaigning hard since this past June, and I had the sense that Glen Pierson was about to start playing dirty as well.

As soon as we finished eating, we headed into the living room to join the others. George, a writer of traditional whodunit mysteries, started off the weekly meeting of the Mystery Mastermind Group at the Gull Island Writers' Retreat with a formal statement of the issue he was presenting.

"Thank you, everyone, for allowing me to speak on behalf of one of our temporary renters, Bosley Newman. Bosley isn't only a fellow author I admire greatly; he's been a good friend for over thirty years. As you all know, Bosley has been working on a historical novel that's based on the history of the lighthouses along the East Coast. The book includes facts relating to each lighthouse, as well as the folklore and legends surrounding each of the ten structures he's highlighting."

We knew all this, but everyone listened politely while George worked through the background. Providing a formal setup, whether it was necessary or not, had become our tradition. "Bosley arrived on Gull Island two weeks ago to research the lighthouse on Skull Island for the seventh chapter in his book. I believe most, if not all of you have had the opportunity to chat with him. The two of us have been getting together every couple of days to discuss his progress. The last time I spoke to him was on Friday of last week. He told me that he'd uncovered an amazing secret that might very well affect some individuals living on Gull Island today. He didn't go into any detail then, but we made plans to meet for lunch on Saturday. He never showed. I left several messages on his cell and have gone by his cabin on numerous occasions since he missed our lunch. In the past, if he's had to cancel plans we've had, he's always called to let me know about it. The fact that he isn't returning my calls has me concerned."

"It sounds like you're worried Bosley has met with foul play," Brit Baxter, writer of chic lit, commented.

"The thought has crossed my mind."

"Do you know where Bosley planned to go on Friday?" I asked as I scooted closer to the crackling fire to ward off a chill I couldn't quite shake. "Did he have interviews set up?"

"He told me that he'd been looking through some old diaries that morning, but he didn't say where he was headed later that afternoon. He might have been following up on the secret he believed he'd uncovered, but he also mentioned earlier in the week that he needed photographs of the lighthouse for the book, so I suppose it's possible he might have rented a boat and gone out to the island. But he may have taken care of the photos earlier in the week and not mentioned it."

"How far away is the island?" I wondered.

"About an hour by boat," George answered.

"Is the lighthouse operational?"

George shook his head. "Not for almost a century."

There was silence in the room as everyone took a minute to digest what he had shared. The cold cases we'd worked on in the past had been relevant to an extent, but other than the missing-sister case we'd worked on over the summer, none had been urgent. A writer who had been missing for a few days did seem to add an element of immediacy.

"How old is this lighthouse exactly?" Jack asked.

My brother, Garrett Hanford, who had recently graduated from a wheelchair to a walker after suffering a stroke, said, "It dates back more than a century, although the island's history goes back farther than that."

Jack raised a brow. "So this secret Bosley was talking about could be centuries old?"

"Perhaps," George answered. "If I had to guess, though, I'd say whatever Bosley found most likely originated within the past hundred years."

"Is the island inhabited?" I asked.

"Not currently," George answered.

"The lighthouse was first built in the early 1800s by English settlers," Meg informed us. "It was manned and operational until the 1920s, although the village was mostly deserted following a devastating hurricane in 1893."

"So the lighthouse keeper lived on the island alone after the village was deserted?" I said.

George nodded. "The accounting of what happened is sketchy, but there are documents that claim he lived alone there over a thirty-year span. There are other stories that state that while the hurricane devastated the island, there were some inhabitants who held fast and stayed to rebuild. I'm not certain of the exact timeline, but, as I said, I know the island is completely deserted now and has been since 1924, when the lighthouse was completely abandoned."

"Why was it abandoned?" Jack inquired.

"It's said the lighthouse was deserted after the last lighthouse keeper died under mysterious circumstances," George explained. "The fact that the term *mysterious circumstances* has been used in relation to the death of this man makes me wonder if the secret Bosley uncovered has something to do with that event."

"So, you're thinking it was Bosley's research that might have gotten him into trouble with someone committed to protecting this secret?" suggested Clara Kline, a writer of paranormal mysteries.

"Perhaps," George said.

"As interesting as this sounds, I'm about to head out on my book tour, so I don't think I'll be able to help out with this one," Alex Cole, a fun and flirty millennial who'd made his first million writing science fiction when he was just twenty-two, informed us. "If you haven't figured things out by the time I get back, I'll jump in then."

"That's fine," I said. "Good luck with the tour. The book's fabulous."

"Thanks. The tour is going to be grueling, but I should be back by Thanksgiving."

"We're planning to do dinner here again," I informed Alex. We'd shared our first holiday meal a year ago, and it looked as if it was going to become a tradition.

"Have you spoken to Rick about your concern about the disappearance of your friend?" Vikki

Vance, my best friend and a romance author, asked George.

"I mentioned it to him, but I don't have enough information to file a missing persons report. At least not yet."

"I can do an internet search to see if he's visited any of the chat rooms he prefers or his social media sites," Brit offered. "I seem to remember him saying he belonged to several chat rooms frequented by academics and historians. If I can find him in any one location, I should be able to map his movements from there. I should also be able to figure out if he's been online since you last spoke to him."

"I'm not sure how I can help with this one, but I'm willing to do whatever you need," Vikki offered. "Gull Island is a small community. It shouldn't be hard to piece together his actions in the days leading up to his disappearance. It sounds as if he was out and about interviewing people."

"He spoke to me on several occasions," Meg said. "I know he also met with Sam Castle, Ron Remand, Zane Carson, and Billy Waller."

"Council members and descendants of the four founding fathers," I said for those who didn't have this piccc of information.

"He asked me about Trout Kellerman a few days back as well," Garrett added.

Kellerman was a fourth-generation fisherman who knew a lot about the area. There were others who had similar backgrounds. I was certain if Bosley had been thorough, the list of men and women he'd interviewed had been extensive.

"Maybe we should put our heads together and come up with a list of people Bosley would most likely have spoken to," Jack suggested. "Once we have it, we can backtrack."

"We should start a whiteboard," I added.

"I'll grab one," Alex offered.

"Thank you, everyone," George said as Alex headed up the stairs to the room we used as a communal den. "I appreciate your help with this matter. As soon as we have our list, we can talk to everyone Bosley might have spoken to. Maybe he said something to someone that will provide a clue as to where he might be now."

I got up and refilled everyone's coffee cups while we waited for Alex to return. Clara had made pumpkin cake with sour cream frosting, and I served that as well. The fire in the kitchen was burning cheerily, providing for a level of warmth that hadn't quite reached the larger living room despite the large stone fireplace that took up almost an entire wall. I loved living in this big old house with Garrett and Clara, but the insulation was pretty much nonexistent, and it got quite drafty during the winter months. I sliced the cake, grabbed some plates, then went back to the living room to serve it.

******

After the meeting broke up, Alex, Brit, and Vikki went back to their cabins, and Garrett and Clara went into the den to watch a movie. George and Meg went out for coffee, and Jack and I took our dog, Kizzy, out for a walk. Jack had recently moved into the cabin he'd built on the south end of the beach. He still owned his mansion on the hill, but he'd said more than once that he intended to sell it once he was settled. The only problem with the three-bedroom, two-bath cabin was that it didn't have a garage. There was outdoor parking for the writers' retreat residents, but Jack had an expensive sports car that really needed to be kept indoors. If he did sell the mansion, where he had the car now, he'd either have to store the car somewhere or sell it.

"What do you think about Bosley's disappearance?" I asked as we drifted from the walkway that wound through the resort to the sandy beach.

Jack slipped his hand into mine. "I'm not sure. The fact that he's missing concerns me. George has known him a long time, and he seems convinced he wouldn't simply disappear. But Brit thinks he might go off on his own and lose track of time. I guess we can't know which it is until we start digging into whatever clues I hope Bosley left for us to follow."

"I hope this isn't too hard on George. He hasn't seemed his usual robust self lately. I almost wonder if he's dealing with a medical issue he isn't talking about."

Jack picked up a stick and tossed it down the beach. Kizzy ran along the waterline, kicking up sand and water as she hurried to retrieve her prize. "I suppose he's getting to the age where health concerns are more common," he agreed. "All we can do is help him as much as we can so the entire burden of finding his friend doesn't fall on his shoulders."

Kizzy rambled up and shook her wet fur all over Jack and me. Then she set the stick at Jack's feet and waited for him to throw it again. Jack obliged. "I wonder if there are any articles about the lighthouse or Skull Island archived in the newspaper's database.

I'll make a note to do a search tomorrow. And I think we should talk to Rick. If nothing else, he should be able to pull any other police reports relating to Skull Island."

"The island has been deserted for almost a century. Do you really think there'll be reports?" I asked.

"I realize there are no residents currently living there, but all the islands in this area attract boat traffic and weekend campers. It's possible there could have been incidents that would have generated reports. If not, at least we'll know nothing really gnarly has occurred there in the past few decades."

I couldn't help but think of other islands nearby where I knew murders and mysterious deaths had occurred. The images in my mind made me cringe.

"I think this little lady is going to need a shower before we let her loose in the cabin," I said when Kizzy ran up, dropped her stick, and rolled in the sand.

"It's a good thing I had the foresight to put an outdoor shower on the deck. We'll rinse her off, then hang out in the kitchen on the tile floor until she dries. I don't want wet dog in my bed again."

"You could make her sleep in her own bed on the floor," I pointed out.

"I could, but I kind of like her keeping my feet warm."

I rolled my eyes. Jack talked the talk, making it seem as if he was the boss in his relationship with the adorable bundle of fur that had captured both our hearts, but it didn't take a genius to see it was Kizzy who ran the show.

Jack called her over and turned on the outdoor shower as soon as we arrived at his place, using the handheld wand to hose her off, then stepped back while she shook. Once she'd gotten rid of most of the water in her coat, he grabbed a towel from the cabinet near the shower and dried her the rest of the way. "I have a bottle of wine. Do you want to come in?" Jack asked.

I hesitated. "I'd love a glass of wine, but it's getting late."

"So stay. We're both going in to the newspaper tomorrow. We can ride there together."

I glanced at the main house, then back at Jack. I stayed over with him on a semiregular basis, so Garrett and Clara knew to lock up if I wasn't home when they went to bed. I had a key if I did come back. "Okay," I agreed. "I guess it would be nice to share a bottle of wine. I wanted to talk to you about the article for the Harvest Festival anyway. I'm meeting Brooke for breakfast to discuss the specifics."

"Will you need a car to meet her?"

I shook my head. "No. We're meeting at the little café just down the street from the newspaper. The festival is going to run Thursday evening through Sunday afternoon, so Brooke wants to be sure we have a big spread on the event. There are several new venues this year, as well as the classics everyone looks forward to."

"I saved pages two and three for the article and photos," Jack informed me. "We'll need to have it formatted by the end of the day tomorrow. I need to follow up on a few things in the morning, but I should be able to work on it in the afternoon."

"Are you still planning to volunteer?"

Jack nodded. "I told Brooke to sign us up for several shifts, as long as we had them at the same time. I'd like to have a chance to take some photos for the newspaper, and maybe interview a few people so we can do a follow-up in the Halloween edition." Jack took my hand in his. "I'd also like time to take in the events with my girl. Last year we were so busy, we didn't really enjoy the festivities."

"I'm really looking forward to this year. I was thinking of doing dinner at the house on Halloween again. I know Alex will be away, but I think everyone else will be around. We can make nachos and watch cheesy horror movies."

"Sounds like fun. We'll need some pumpkins to carve."

"We can pick some up this week. I want to stop by the dime store to pick up some little gifts to send to Abby and her kids."

Abby Boston was a young widow raising five children. The Mastermind group had sort of adopted her and her children during her pregnancy with her daughter, Tammy. After the baby was born and Abby had been able to collect the life insurance money her husband, who had been a firefighter, had provided for her, Jack had helped her out with a down payment on a house in Georgia, where she had two cousins and an aunt. Abby and her children seemed to be doing well and didn't actually need our help any longer, but everyone had grown fond of the little family, and we all sent gifts from time to time.

"It looks like you have a call." I nodded to Jack's phone, which was on silent but was vibrating.

Jack picked it up, looked at the caller ID, and answered. "Jack Jones." Jack's smile turned into a frown as he listened to whoever was on the other end of the line. "Okay. I'll be right there. And no, don't bother to call him. I'll take care of it."

"What was that all about?" I asked as Jack hung up.

"That was the new deputy working under Rick. I think his name is Kyle. He called to inform me that a body washed up on the shore just north of here."

"They called so you could cover it for the newspaper?" I asked.

Jack nodded. "They also wanted to know if they should call George."

I gasped. "Bosley?"

"I'm afraid so."

Chapter 2

Tuesday, October 23

Brooke Johnson was a go-getter and the event chairperson for the island. I'd first met her shortly after arriving here to help Garrett with the remodel of the resort after he suffered the stroke and was hospitalized. Brooke was one of the suspects and one of the witnesses in the very first cold case mystery the group and I had investigated after the Gull Island Writers' Retreat was established. While things had turned out all right, it was touch-and-go for her for a while. I think she appreciated the fact that Jack and I, along with the other writers, had gone out of our way to help her. We'd been friends ever since.

"Sorry I'm late," Brooke said as she rushed into the café, where I was nursing a cup of coffee. "My oldest forgot her lunch, so even though I had a substitute taking over my class so I could take the day off to firm up everything for the festival, I had to run over to the school. Of course, once I got there, it seemed everyone had a question that couldn't wait until tomorrow, so I was trapped in the hallway outside the main office for a lot longer than I planned."

"It's not a problem at all," I said. "I really admire the way you juggle a husband, three children, a career in teaching, and also manage to oversee most of the events the island sponsors. I've pretty much decided you must not sleep."

"Sleep?" Brooke chuckled.

I smiled. "A rare commodity in your life, I'm sure."

She took off her jacket and tossed it onto the seat of the booth, then slid in next to it. "Before we start talking Harvest Festival, catch me up on what happened to that writer who's been staying out at your place. I heard his body was found washed up on the beach."

I had to hand it to the Gull Island gossip hotline. They were fast. Of course, Brooke was well connected, so I was sure she was one of the first to hear the news when there was something scandalous going on. "His name was Bosley Newman. He was a friend of George's and had been on the island for about two weeks, researching the lighthouse on Skull Island for a book he was writing."

"So how did he end up dead?" Brooke asked as she motioned for a waitress to bring her a cup of coffee.

"We aren't sure yet. Bosley told George he'd stumbled on a secret that, while not recently established, could have ramifications in the present."

Brooke wrinkled her nose. "Secrets can be nasty things. Hard to keep and even harder to deal with when they finally come to light. Trust me, I know that to be true."

I tilted my head. "I know you do. So far, we don't know anything about it other than that Bosley had come across one."

"Wow. I'm so very sorry. And I'm so sorry for George. I know how hard it is too lose a friend. Is there anything I can do?"

I shook my head. "I don't think so. Unless you know something about the history of Skull Island?"

Brooke leaned forward, resting her arms on the table. "I'm not sure exactly how events correspond with specific dates, but I do know the place served as the location of more than one bloodbath in its history."

I scrunched my nose. "Bloodbath?"

Brooke nodded, then took a sip of the coffee the waitress set down in front of her. "Based on what I've heard along the way, I believe the island was initially occupied by an indigenous people. Then, at some point, some pirates came along and massacred them to take over and build their own settlement. The pirates lived there for a while but were eventually chased away by the Spanish settlers who came to the area to build missions all up and down the southern part of the East Coast. This happened centuries ago. The Spanish left when the English arrived. I'm pretty sure every time the place changed hands, blood was shed. They say the island is haunted, and I don't doubt it. Do you think something that happened there is behind the death of George's friend?"

I leaned back against the booth. "I don't know. At this point, no one knows what happened. Bosley's body was washed up on the beach, so it looks like it most likely was dumped from a boat. Rick is still waiting for the medical examiner's report to determine time of death and whether he died as a result of drowning or was killed prior to being dumped into the ocean."

"When was the last time anyone saw or spoke to him?" Brooke asked.

"Friday. At least, that's the last time anyone from the resort spoke to him. George is spending the morning going through the notes Bosley left in his cabin. Then he's going to try to create a timeline that will show us where he went and to whom he spoke. Once we get a list of people to talk to, I guess we'll start asking questions and see where that takes us."

Brooke put her hand over mine. "If I can do anything, don't hesitate to ask."

"Thank you. Listen, I know your schedule is tight today, so we should probably get to what we came here to discuss. I brought a rough sketch of the way I envision the layout looking. I dug out photos from some of the harvest festivals in the past to give some excitement and color to the spread."

"That's great," Brooke said. "I have the articles I promised you all written, but feel free to edit them as needed. My main objective is to get island folks as well as people in the greater area to come to the event in droves. The school can really use a boost to the budget this fund-raiser provides."

"We're going to feature the festival on our website, and Jack and I are both planning to volunteer wherever you need us."

"That's great, because I have you both scheduled for the haunted house on Friday evening and the kiddie carnival on Saturday morning. I'm hoping to have enough volunteers so that each shift will only be around four hours. The haunted house runs from five to nine on Friday, so that's a four-hour shift already. I'll e-mail you the details."

"Okay, I'll look for it. Are you moving the haunted house to the wharf, as we discussed at the planning meeting?"

Brooke nodded. "We are. I hope the weather holds, because the wharf won't be a good place to be during a storm."

"I think there's supposed to be a storm rolling in this afternoon, but it should blow through by Thursday morning."

Brooke let out a breath. "That's good. The volunteer who's organizing the haunted house wants to do an indoor/outdoor thing. The guests will first walk through a haunted graveyard that zigzags along the wharf, then the actual haunted house will be set up in the old cannery at the end of the wharf. The cannery has a spooky feeling, even without the decorations. When the place is decked out with terrifying monsters and things that jump out and startle you, it's going to be amazing."

"I bet. I can't wait."

Brooke and I spent the next hour eating and discussing the specific highlights and updates to the event. As always, Brooke had put a lot of thought into every aspect of the four-day celebration, and I could tell it was going to be awesome. I'd had a blast last year, and despite the investigation into Bosley's death, which I knew would most likely become completely engrossing, I was looking forward to my volunteer duties. Brooke and I chatted a while longer, then she returned to her list of errands and I went to the newspaper. As I came up, I saw Jack had strung orange lights in the window while I was with Brooke. There were fall leaves and shiny orange pumpkins on the counter as well.

"Wow, the place looks greats," I said to Jack after greeting Kizzy, who acted like she hadn't seen me in a month.

"I figured with most of the businesses in town decorating, we should too. I wanted to get a skeleton for the door, but the Halloween shop was out of them. I might go back later to take a look around for an alternative. That is, if we have time. I have a feeling this is going to be a busy day."

"Have you heard from George?" I wondered.

"No, but I did hear from Rick. According to the ME, Bosley died between nine p.m. on Friday and four a.m. on Saturday. The official cause of death is a blow to the head. It appears he was already dead when he went into the water. Rick doesn't have any idea where the murder occurred or who might have killed him yet, but he's highly motivated to find out and actually asked if we want to help with the long list of interviews that need to be conducted."

That was a switch. While Rick had been pretty good about working with us in the past, it was usually us who went to him with the request to be involved. "I'm certainly willing to help out. Do we have a list to start from?"

"George and Rick got together and went over the notes Bosley left in his cabin. They've compiled a list from them. Given that Bosley was here to do research, the list is fairly extensive. We don't know what the secret he alluded to was, so all the people mentioned in Bosley's notes seem equally likely to have had a conflict with him."

"Maybe, but not everyone on the list can be equally likely to kill someone," I said.

"That has to be true, which is why we're meeting Rick to discuss the list. He suggested we grab lunch. I told him we'd meet him at Gertie's at one."

"Luckily, I only had a muffin and coffee when I met Brooke. I have her notes and articles, by the way. I'll work on formatting everything she gave us while you finish what you're doing."

"I'm almost done here. Did Brooke say when she needed us to work?"

"Friday evening for the haunted house and Saturday morning for the kiddie carnival. She's going to e-mail a schedule and instructions. Did you hear they were going to move the haunted house to the old cannery on the wharf?"

"I did hear some chatter about that. It's a spooky location. I just hope they had someone go through the place to check for safety issues. I'm pretty sure the building has been vacant for quite some time."

"Brooke is very thorough; I'm sure she thought of that. The biggest issue in her mind was the weather, because there's an outdoor component." I brought the page layout up on the large monitor, then made a few adjustments. Brooke's articles were a tad on the long side, so I'd need to do some editing to get everything to fit. Overall, however, the two-page spread was going to look awesome. I felt certain the *Gull Island News* could help attract the visitors the community hoped for.

"Was the ad for the weekly specials sent over from the market?" Jack asked.

"Yeah. It was in the in-box when I looked earlier. The Halloween shop sent ad material as well. They're having a blowout this weekend, which makes sense if you don't want to store inventory until next year. We should be able to finish the formatting for tomorrow's run before we meet Rick. I just have a few edits to make with this layout; then I can start on the ads."

"Don't forget to include the information the shelter sent over about the dog parade."

"I left room for it on page five. Maybe we should enter Kizzy."

Jack paused, as if to give the idea some thought. "It would be fun for her, but we'll have to look at the timing of the parade and compare it to our other volunteer duties. I think the parade is on Saturday morning, and you just said we were scheduled to work the kiddie carnival then."

"I suppose I can ask Brit or Vikki if they want to do the parade with Kizzy. Not that she'll care if she misses it, but it would be fun to dress her up and let her strut her stuff."

"We'll see if we can work it out." Jack held up a photo.

"What's that?"

"One of the photos I took at the house fire last night. It was small and did minimal damage, but as I mentioned, it seemed to have been intentionally set, so there's an active investigation."

"I hope they catch whoever's behind these fires soon."

"I do too. In general, an arsonist working an area is a cause for great alarm, but there's something odd about the way these fires don't seem to be set to do much damage to property."

"Why bother to set a fire if you aren't trying to burn something down?"

"Maybe this arsonist is just really bad at it, but it's more likely the minimal damage is intentional."

"Maybe it's just a bunch of kids messing around."

Jack shrugged. "Maybe. Let's get that layout uploaded."

******

By the time one o'clock rolled around, the newspaper was formatted and ready to print and I was starving, which was a good thing because Gertie's on the Wharf is one of my favorite places to eat. Like the other business owners in town, Gertie had decorated her place with colorful leaves, bright orange pumpkins, and seasonal accents that made her customers feel right at home. Rick had arrived ahead of us and was sipping a cola while he looked at the menu. I planned to have hot pastrami with a cup of soup, which seemed perfect on a blustery day.

"Storms comin'," Gertie said as she delivered a coffeepot to our table. "I heard we're supposed to get a significant amount of rain. I'm hopin' it'll move through before the festival opens on Thursday night. A lot of people have worked really hard on it; I'd hate to see it have to be canceled."

"The storm's supposed to blow in this evening and blow out by Thursday morning," Rick said. "If it does rain this weekend, it won't be the first time they've had to move things inside. Not that an indoor event is preferable, but it's possible."

"It might be possible, but it would cut down greatly on attendance," I pointed out.

"If there's one thing you can't control, it's the weather." Rick shrugged.

Rick was right. Worrying about rain wasn't going to change a darn thing.

"I heard about your renter," Gertie said to me after filling our water glasses. "Any idea who's responsible for that poor man's death?"

I glanced at Rick. "That's what we're here to discuss."

Gertie tapped her pencil on her order pad. "Uh-huh. That's what I figured. I met him once or twice. Seemed nice enough. A little scatterbrained at times, but nice all the same. I sure do hope you find out who did it. It just isn't right."

"Seems you have quite a bit of information given the fact that I haven't yet provided any details to the public or made an official statement," Rick said.

"You know ol' Gertie has her ways of knowin' what there is to know. Now, what can I get y'all for lunch?"

We placed our orders and Gertie went to the kitchen to prepare our meals, and Rick handed Jack and me each a sheet of paper. "George and I came up with a list of people Bosley spoke to or planned to speak to. Unfortunately, that amounts to a lot of people. We tried to prioritize; the names at the top of the list are the people who might have a stake in something that happened during the time period Bosley seemed to be focused on, which as near as we can tell, is between the hurricane of 1893 and the desertion of the island after the last lighthouse keeper died."

The list had some predictable names: Sam Castle, Ron Remand, Zane Carson, and Billy Waller, all of them descended from men and women who'd lived on Gull Island back then. There were also people who seemed to me to have less obvious links, such as Pastor Blaine Branderman of the Gull Island Community Church and Buck Johnston, a commercial fisherman.

"Why are Pastor Branderman and Buck Johnston on the list?" I asked.

"According to Bosley's phone records, he called the Gull Island Community Church seven times during the past two weeks. I spoke to Pastor Branderman, who said Bosley had visited the church four times in the past week. Bosley was interested in looking at old documents that have been stored in a secure room in the basement since the church was built. George and I think there might be church records that will help us determine what Bosley was up to. As for Buck Johnston, he's a fourth-generation fisherman in the area, like Trout Kellerman and Tizzy Tizdale. None of them would have been born yet, but they might have photos, diaries, or family histories that could shed some light on what Bosley had latched on to."

"Are you sure the years between the hurricane and the death of the last lighthouse keeper in 1924 is the relevant timespan?" Jack asked. "It was my understanding that Bosley was researching the entire history of the lighthouse."

Rick took another sip of his cola before answering. "While we didn't find anything that unequivocally states what time period Bosley was focused on, it does seem that after he completed a general overview of the entire span of time, he focused on the thirty-one years we've identified as most likely to be relevant. We have a lot of ground to cover because we don't know what he was interested in, so starting off by speaking to folks who had a connection to the island as far back as the 1890s seemed like a good way to narrow things down."

We paused our conversation when Gertie brought us our lunch. She stayed with us for a few minutes while she made sure we had everything we needed, then went to help another customer who'd just come in.

"So, who do you want us to speak to?" I asked.

"I'd like you to start at the church. Pastor Branderman is expecting you and has agreed to give you access to the same documents Bosley was interested in. I'm hoping something will jump out and provide us with a motive."

"Sounds fine," Jack agreed. "Although digging through a room full of old documents seems more like a George thing."

"George drove down to Savannah to talk to another writer friend Bosley confided in and went to for help. Brit offered to go with him so he didn't have to drive alone with the storm coming. They won't be back until late tonight or even tomorrow, so I thought the two of you could start on the church documents. George seemed to think it was important to figure out what he found in the church."

******

After lunch, Jack and I went back to the newspaper. We'd brought Kizzy to work with us, so she'd been waiting for our return. We dropped her off at his cabin before we headed to the church, which was a good call because we ended up being there for the rest of the afternoon. Pastor Branderman didn't know what Bosley had uncovered, but he'd spent several days going through the diaries, photos, and church records in the basement room. It was the pastor's opinion that Bosley was excited about whatever he'd stumbled upon.

"There are a lot of really interesting things down here," I said after we'd been at it for at least two hours. "Not only are there all these old books and handwritten journals, but there are letters, baptism, marriage, and death certificates, and tons of old photos. I know we don't have a lot of time, but I bet we can use some of the information in here to run a compelling historical account of the island as a community interest piece. Maybe even a series of articles that look back at the events that shaped its destiny."

"I like the idea," Jack said. He paused and set the pile of photos he'd been looking through to the side. "The problem we have today, however, is the sheer volume of data in this room. Everything seems interesting and possibly even relevant, but I haven't come across anything I'd consider shocking."

"Yeah." I stood up and stretched. "Even if we did come across a photo or journal entry that might prove to be scandalous, we wouldn't know what we were looking at without a frame of reference."

Jack sat back in his chair and stretched out his legs. "It stands to reason that if Bosley found something scandalous, he would have notes about it, even if they were vague. Even if he only jotted down a few sentences to remind himself of something he wanted to research further or maybe verify. Rick said he and George went through the notes they found in Bosley's cabin, but what if he had notes someplace else? Somewhere hidden, perhaps."

"Makes sense. He probably wouldn't leave important notes just sitting on his desk for anyone to find. But where would he hide them?"

Jack frowned. "Rick said he called the church on multiple occasions, but he didn't mention what other numbers he might have called during the same time. It might be a good idea for him to take a look at all Bosley's phone records. Do we know if his cell phone was found?"

I shook my head. "His phone wasn't found on him, nor was it in his cabin or his car. The GPS locator isn't working, which means the phone is either turned off or it's been destroyed."

"It's probably at the bottom of the ocean," Jack said.

I looked up from the file I'd begun to thumb through. "Probably. His computer is also missing, although George did say Bosley backed everything up online. Of course, that won't do us any good unless we can find the storage provider and the password. George is working on that, but he wasn't confident about his ability to get into the file when I spoke to him. Our best bet is probably still trying to figure out where he'd been and who he spoke to."

Jack stood up and began to walk around the room. We'd been working for a long time. I really needed to stretch as well. He paced across the room and then back again, deep in thought. Eventually, he said, "Maybe we're going at this the wrong way. We're focusing on trying to figure out the content of Bosley's research, but maybe we should be trying to figure out who he's been with and who had the opportunity to kill him. If he was dumped in the ocean, that means he must have been on a boat at some point. Maybe we should head over to the marina. It's a busy place. Someone must have seen something."

I bit my lip, tilting my head slightly as I considered that. "Maybe. The marina has security cameras to provide protection for the expensive boats docked there, but they would also record who was around. If Bosley was dumped from a boat that had been docked at the marina, we should be able to find out which one he boarded and with whom, but I'm sure Rick must be checking on that. The reality is, there are vessels secured to private docks all over the island. If someone used one of those boats to take Bosley out to sea, there wouldn't be a record of it."

"It makes sense that anyone who docked at the marina would know about the cameras and avoid it for that reason."

"I think the killer must have used a private boat. According to Rick and the ME, Bosley would have been killed sometime after dark on Friday. It would be easy to sneak him into a private boat and then dump him, assuming he was already dead. Of course, I suppose a boat would be a good place to kill someone as well, so that might also be where he died."

Jack nodded. "If the boat was out to sea, there'd be no one around to hear him scream."

The very idea of that was making me queasy. I couldn't understand what sort of a person would kill someone else no matter what the circumstances. I glanced at Jack, who was now engrossed in a ledger he'd sat back down to look through. "Did you find something?"

Jack glanced up at me. "Maybe." He flipped through a few more pages, frowning all the while. The ledger appeared to be old, the cover made of leather from what I could see, the pages yellowed with age.

"Maybe?" I asked. "Can you be a bit more specific?"

"Sorry. This appears to be some kind of directory. There are names recorded chronologically by either date of birth or the date an individual moved into the community the book was created to document. I'm not sure if the list relates to members of the church, or perhaps of the community as a whole."

"So it's a record of first arrival?"

"And more," Jack corrected. "The initiating factor to be entered into the ledger seems to be birth or arrival, but there are other columns as well. There's an entry if the person was baptized, married, or had children. There's also a column for the date of their death."

"Is it a recent list?" I asked.

Jack shook his head. "No. This covers people who were born in the late 1800s and early 1900s." He turned back to the first page. "The first entry is Jeremiah Jensen, who was born on January 2, 1875. He was baptized on March 8, married on June 15, 1902, and died on December 4, 1913." Jack turned to the back of the book. "The last entry is for a Caroline Barrington. She was born on December 28, 1924.

There's no record of anything other than her birth: no marriage or death."

"So they only kept records during this fifty-year span?"

"Probably not. I assume there are other registers just like this one for the important events in the lives of individuals born before and after. I don't know why the last few entries end with people's birth. Maybe whoever kept the register updated stopped doing it in 1924. What I find interesting isn't the continuity of the records but a recurring date: November 12, 1924."

"What do you mean? Were a bunch of people born on that date?"

"No. That's when a bunch of people died."

Chapter 3

It was pouring rain when we left the church. We stopped by the newspaper to do a search for November 12, 1924, to see if there had been some cataclysmic event on that date that would explain a rash of deaths. Despite an exhaustive search, we were unable to find anything on either the local newspaper websites or in the sites of some of the larger newspapers around the country. Then we called Meg, who was full of information on local history. She couldn't think of anything offhand but promised to do some looking in to it.

Jack and I had no way of knowing whether whatever had happened on November 12, 1924, was relevant to Bosley's death, so we didn't want to spend a ton of time on it. We didn't find anything else that seemed important at the church, but there was a ton of material to go through, so we planned to go back to the basement after we got the paper out tomorrow morning.

"I'd suggest we stop for dinner, but with the rain coming down this way, it's probably better to go out to the resort," Jack said as we left the newspaper.

I jumped as a bolt of lightning streaked across the sky. "Yikes. That was close."

"Too close," Jack said as a rolling boom of thunder followed immediately after.

"I guess we should have gone back to the resort earlier. The rain's really coming down. Can you see the road?"

"I can, but just barely." Jack slowed the truck as he neared a low spot in the road. "It looks like the coast road is flooded. We'll need to circle back around and take the marsh road. It'll add fifteen minutes to the trip, but I don't think it's a good idea to cross here. It's hard to tell exactly how deep the water is."

"I'm sure you're right," I said as the vibration following a clap of thunder shook the truck.

I held on to the door handle as Jack slowly negotiated a U-turn. I'd hoped the rain would have let up by this point, but so far it was coming down in sheets that hit the already saturated earth. I actually liked storms, even ones with thunder and lightning, but the strikes from this storm were a bit too close for comfort, especially because we appeared to be the only vehicle on the road.

I turned and looked at him. "If the coast road from town is flooded, I wonder if the resort road is flooded too. There's that one low spot that always floods during heavy rain, especially if it comes during high tide."

Jack clutched the steering wheel with both hands. "I guess all we can do now is go on. If the road is flooded, we'll head to my house on the bluff. Most of my stuff is still there, and I seem to remember a lot of your things are there as well. Kizzy is at the resort, but I'm sure Garrett and Clara won't mind keeping her overnight if they need to."

"They won't mind. Blackbeard, on the other hand, might have a fit," I said, referring to Garrett's parrot, who wasn't at all fond of the energetic puppy.

The road circled back and hugged the coastline, before it headed inland toward the marsh on the opposite side of the island. I looked out my window as giant waves crashed onto the shore. I'd only lived on the island for a little over a year, but the waves tonight could very well be the biggest I'd ever seen along this stretch. The resort was protected by a reef, but with the tide that was going on tonight, I worried about the cabins closest to the waterline.

"The wind is going to play havoc with the decorations in town," Jack commented.

"As well as the ones a lot of folks have put up in their yards. I hope that house on Elm with all the giant blow-up ghosts took them down. Otherwise, I'm afraid they'll be flying through the air tonight."

Jack slowed to avoid a lawn chair that blew across the road. "Where on earth did that come from?" he said. "There aren't any houses for at least a quarter mile."

"The wind might have carried it quite a ways." I squinted into the distance. "What's that over there?" I pointed to a light that seemed to be reflecting off the clouds.

Jack frowned. "It looks like a spotlight. Perhaps from a boat?"

"Anyone out in a boat tonight would have to be crazy. Besides, it looks as if it's coming from someplace closer to shore. Maybe even on the beach."

"Once we get around this next set of curves we should be able to get a better look at it."

I tried to focus on the light through the pounding rain. It was moving to and fro, as if the source of the light was being tossed around. Maybe it was a boat. "There." I pointed at an object just beyond the edge of the beach."

"It's a car," Jack said, pulling over to the side of the road. "I'm going to check it out. Call Rick. If he doesn't answer right away, call 911."

"Be careful," I called after him as he opened his door, struggling to keep it from blowing clean off its hinges. After he closed the door, he bent his head and trudged through the heavy rain to the car, which appeared to be drifting farther and farther out to sea.

I called Rick as a flash of lightning illuminated the sky less than a second before the crash of thunder vibrated around me. I hated the fact that Jack was out in the storm and wanted to call him back, but if there was someone in the car…

"There's been an accident," I said to Rick as soon as he answered. "Jack and I are on the coast road maybe halfway between town and the resort road, at the spot where the road hugs the coast before heading inland. The road is flooded farther down toward the resort road, so we were trying to loop back around. I don't know if anyone is in the car. Jack went to check."

"I'm on my way. The fire department will probably beat me to your location, so keep an eye out for them."

I switched on the truck flashers before I turned my attention to the door handle next to me. The rain was coming down so hard, I couldn't see Jack from where I was sitting, but I anticipated he might need help. It took me a few tries to get the door open with the force of the wind pushing against it, but eventually, I was able to slip out into the rain.

"Damn."

Talk about a hurricane. Okay, so the weather service wasn't labeling it as such, but I didn't want to be anywhere near the island if the real thing ever headed this way.

I could see Jack as he waded into the water despite the huge waves crashing around him. The car was close to being under now, so if there was anyone inside, we didn't have long to get them out before it was washed out to sea.

"Is there someone inside?" I called to Jack, who was standing chest-deep in water.

"The driver," Jack called back as I began to wade to him. The surge from the sea was strong, and I was only an okay swimmer. I hoped I wasn't the one who ended up being washed away.

"Is he okay?" I yelled back.

"Slumped over the wheel. I don't even know if he's still alive. He hasn't responded to my attempts to communicate so far. Is help on the way?"

"Yes, and Rick's sending the fire department as well. They're closer, so those sirens in the distance are probably them." I jumped as lightning flashed overhead. "We really shouldn't be in this water."

"Yeah." Jack began wading back toward me. "I can't get the door open anyway. We'll need to find something to break the window."

"Do you know who it is?" I asked as we struggled through the churning water back to the beach.

"I couldn't see his face, but based on the car he's driving and his overall build, I think it might be Billy Waller."

I ran my hands over my face in an attempt to wipe away my drenched hair. "I wonder how he ended up in the water."

"The back of the vehicle is totally smashed in. I think he was run off the road. If no one called it in or stayed around to help, I'm thinking it might have been intentional."

Although Billy Waller was another descendent of one of the founding fathers, he wasn't involved in politics the way Sam was. Still, he wielded a certain amount of power on the island based on lineage alone. If someone had intentionally run Billy off the road just the day after Bosley's body was found on the beach, I'd say it was highly suspect.

"We need to find a big rock or something to break a window," Jack said.

I looked around, but all I could see was dark sky, pouring rain, and white sand. "This stretch is pretty free of rocks or anything else. Maybe the tire iron from the truck?"

"That might work, although I can see the lights from the emergency vehicles," Jack said. "They'll probably be here before we can get back to the truck to get the tire iron. The car is drifting, but the waves are both pulling it out and pushing it back to the beach. I think it'll be okay for a few minutes. Let's go up and fill them in."

It took Rick, Jack, and the four firemen who'd responded to the 911 call working together to pull

Billy from the vehicle. He wasn't washed out to sea as we'd feared, and he didn't drown, but, unfortunately, he didn't make it either. By the time we made it back to the resort, the thunder and lightning had passed, and the rain had slowed to a drizzle. The forecast was for rain to continue through the night, but from what I could see, the worst of the storm was behind us.

"More coffee?" Vikki asked.

"Please," I answered. When Jack and I had returned to the resort, we'd gone to his place, showered, and changed into dry clothes before heading to the main house to collect Kizzy. Vikki, Garrett, and Clara were all there, so we sat down at the kitchen table and caught everyone up while Clara scrambled us some eggs.

"I just don't understand who would run poor Billy off the road that way," Garrett said. "He's a nice man who's done a lot to give back to the community. In fact, of all the descendants of the founding fathers, Billy's the nicest. And he's definitely the most genuine of the bunch. Sam Castle is all about politics, Ron Remand only seems to care about spending his grandpappy's money, and Zane Carson seems to be a lot more interested in preserving the historical purity of the island than he is about working for and with the people who live here."

"What do you mean by that?" I asked.

"Zane is proud of his heritage and the place in local society his lineage provides for him, which is fine; I get that. If I was descended from a founding father, I'd be proud as well. But there have been times when preserving what's always been has gotten in the way of doing what needs to be done now."

I frowned as I tried to follow this line of thought.

"For example," Garrett continued, "a while back, a man named Gordon Ringwald passed away. Gordon had lived on the island for a long time and wanted to give back to the community, so he left money in his will to build new ball fields for both adult and youth sports programs. Most considered that a very generous and timely gift. The island didn't have any ball fields at all, and the local leagues had to travel to fields on the next island over to practice."

"Sounds like a nice gift."

"It was." Garrett nodded. "The land that was identified for use was out near the recreation complex on the south end of the island. It was a large piece of property, and almost everyone agreed it was the perfect location. The problem was that there was a statue of the four founding fathers on the beach near where the ball fields were going to be. Zane was concerned that a foul baseball or a stray kick of a soccer ball would damage the statue, which had been erected to memorialize the exact spot it was believed the four men landed when they first came to settle the island. Zane actually went so far as to retain an attorney to block the project. Members of the community tried to offer reasonable alternatives— moving the statue to another location or building a fence around it—but Zane wouldn't hear of it."

"So what happened?"

"Eventually, the committee in charge gave up. An alternate location was found, although the land we ended up using wasn't as large, nor was it near the recreation complex, making it harder for the summer kids' leagues to use. A lot of folks are still grumbling about it. Zane didn't own that first piece of land, and a lot of folks didn't think he should have had a say in the whole thing."

"Who does own that land?" I asked.

"The town. It's still sitting empty. Personally, I didn't care about the ball fields one way or another. It wasn't like I was going to play sports after I'd reached a certain age. But I didn't think the wishes of one man should prevail over the needs of the many."

"Has the spot been deemed a historical site?" Jack asked.

Garrett shook his head. "Although the statue was erected as a memorial of sorts, there's no proof that stretch of beach is even the actual place where the founding fathers landed."

I could understand how one might want to preserve a piece of history, but if the site hadn't even been authenticated, I didn't see the harm in moving the statue.

"How did Billy feel about the statue?" I asked.

"He supported moving it up to the museum," Garrett answered.

"You don't think Zane ran him off the road, do you?" I asked.

Garrett raised a brow. "Over a statue? No, I don't think even Zane would stoop that low. Besides, the issue was resolved when the fields were built elsewhere. I just used this as an example of Zane being difficult at times. I can't think of a single person who would have intentionally run Billy off the road."

"Maybe not, but it appears that's what someone did."

******

Later that evening, Jack, Kizzy, and I went back to his cabin. The wind had stilled and the rain was nothing more than a drizzle, though the waves outside were still quite a bit larger than normal. I was willing to bet they'd be gently rolling onto the shore by morning.

The cabin Jack had built was both roomy and cozy, a two-story structure with a large living space including a gourmet kitchen and a seating area on the first floor, and three bedrooms and two baths upstairs. A bedroom and attached bath at the back of the cabin that overlooked the sea was his master suite, while he'd turned the middle bedroom into an office, and the extra room at the front of the cabin was currently unfurnished but would become a guest room.

Jack built a fire in the brick fireplace while I poured us each a glass of wine. I was still a little shaky after our attempted water rescue in the middle of an intense lightning storm. Leaving the truck hadn't been a good idea, but really, what else were we to do? We didn't know Billy was already dead, so we had no choice but to try to help him out of the vehicle. I couldn't help but shudder when I considered the many ways our attempted rescue could have ended up even more tragic than it already was.

"This is nice," I said after he sat down next to me on the sofa. I sipped my wine and watched the flames as they reflected off the shiny wood floor. Every now and then, a crash from the waves outside the large picture window penetrated the room, which Jack had left dark except for the fire and a few candles scattered about.

"It's hard to relax, but I have to agree, this is nice."

Kizzy jumped up onto the sofa and cuddled next to Jack. She put her head in his lap, and Jack ran his hand through her fur as we both let our tension drift away. I'd never had a pet before Kizzy. Not that she was mine, though Jack and I were supposed to be sharing her, so I considered her part mine, though she spent most of her time with him. Before Kizzy came into our lives, I'd never considered how much a pet can add to your mental health. Spending time with Kizzy was the greatest stress reliever I'd ever known. Well, almost.

"You know," Jack said, "if you moved in with me, we could end every evening this way."

"Even when it's so God-awful hot you feel like your skin is going to melt right off your body?"

"Well, no, I guess we wouldn't have a fire on nights like that. But I plan to build a deck in the back, overlooking the sea. It would be nice to sit out there on the hot nights."

I did love Jack, and this was very nice, and now that he had a cabin mere steps away from the house I currently called home, I didn't suppose I had a huge reason to say no. Yet I found myself hesitating.

"If you aren't careful, you're going to overwhelm Kizzy with your enthusiasm," he teased.

I smiled. "I'm sorry. I feel as if I need some time to think about your suggestion. You know I love you, and this house is great. And the way things are going between Garrett and Clara, I can see them wanting to have the big house to themselves at some point. But I also feel living together is a big step. We already work together, which means we're together most of the time as it is. What if we get sick of each other?"

Jack ran a finger down my arm. "I'm not going to get sick of you. Are you worried you're going to get sick of me?"

I sighed. "No. Probably not. But maybe. I think it would be remiss of us not to consider there could be a maybe."

Jack nodded slightly. "Okay. How about this: we'll experiment and see how it goes. Bring some clothes over, as well as anything else you feel you might need, and stay with me here for two weeks. That means coming home to this house with me, spending the night here, and planning a life in this house with me. For two weeks. At the end of that, we can see how it went and maybe talk about a permanent arrangement."

"What if we get into a fight?"

"Couples do fight from time to time. I think we'll survive. And if we don't, for the two-week trial at least, you still have your room in the big house to go back to."

I'm not sure why it is I'm not a fan of big decisions, big changes, or big commitments, but for some reason, I was finding all three terrified me. At least they did when it came to Jack. Maybe I began to cower in fear whenever he talked about taking our relationship and shaking things up a bit because it meant so much to me.

"I guess I could spend the next two weeks here with you, but we aren't living together."

"Got it. We'll be overnight pals, but we aren't living together."

"And if Garrett has a relapse and needs me, or things get too intense and one or both of us needs some space, I'll go back to the big house with no hurt feelings and no regrets."

"There are bound to be regrets," Jack pointed out. "But I can agree that if it doesn't work out, we'll continue on as we are now and not let it destroy what we already have."

I took a deep breath and let it out slowly. "Okay. I'll live with you here for two weeks beginning tomorrow."

Jack's face fell just a bit. "Tomorrow?"

"I need time to pack before I can move in for the trial, but I wouldn't be averse to staying over tonight as a guest, not a roommate."

Jack set down his wine. He took mine and set it down as well. Then he nudged Kizzy aside a bit as he pulled me into his arms.

Chapter 4

Wednesday, October 24

It took us most of the morning to get the paper printed and distributed to the vendors who stocked it for distribution to their customers. We also had an online edition with a much larger readership than the hard copy, which was purchased by locals who made the trip to the newspaper rack most Wednesday afternoons. The paper no longer offered home delivery, which I was afraid was a quickly dying concept, but we continued to print it for those who liked to hold the paper and smell the ink.

The rain that had tapered off the previous evening was back. I'd hoped the storm would have blown over completely, but no such luck. The last thing I wanted to do was spend any more time outdoors in the rain than was necessary, but we did have a mystery to solve, and I'd just as soon do that sooner rather than later. Rick had called to let us know our meeting with him and George had been moved to the museum so Meg could join the discussion as well. With all the rain, no one was thinking about touring the facility, so there was very little chance we'd be disturbed.

"It's really coming down," I said to Jack as we drove through the little town toward the museum. Even with the rain, I was enjoying the seasonal decorations that had either survived yesterday's wind or been repaired and rehung.

"According to the weather report, the precipitation should lighten by midafternoon and be gone by tomorrow morning," Jack assured me.

"At least the wind and lightning are gone."

"There is that," Jack agreed. "If it does let up as predicted, I thought we'd head back to the church for a few hours after we finish with Rick, George, and Meg. That November date I discovered has really grabbed hold of me. I'd like the opportunity to dig a little deeper."

"It occurred to me that what caused all those deaths might be related to the death of the last lighthouse keeper," I said. "I don't remember anyone specifying when he died, but I do remember it was in 1924."

Jack tilted his head slightly, though he continued to focus on the road. "I hadn't put that together. Maybe the mysterious circumstances under which the man died are related to a whole lot of deaths and not just the one. We should be able to find out more about the last lighthouse keeper's death if we take the time to do some digging. There are not only records going back that far but there seems to be a certain amount of legend associated with it."

"Do you think Billy's death is related to whatever happened to Bosley?" I asked.

Jack shrugged. "Maybe, though it seems like a long shot."

When we arrived at the museum, George, Rick, and Meg were already deep into a conversation about information George had received from the writer he'd visited. Meg offered us orange tea and pumpkin muffins, which we both accepted, then Rick caught us up on what we'd missed.

"Bosley not only had been sharing his notes and ideas with George," Rick informed us, "but with his friend Tom as well. Tom lives in Savannah, which is where George was yesterday. Most of what Tom received from Bosley was the same thing he told George, but he also mailed a package to Tom on Friday, which he received yesterday. Both Tom and George believe Bosley planned to provide that material to George when they met on Saturday."

"What was in the package?" I asked.

"A file with notes and photos," George said. "The photos are old, at least fifty or sixty years or even more. The notes are copies of a document that was originally created using some type of shorthand. I haven't had the opportunity to try to decode it yet."

"Why would Bosley send his friend a file he couldn't read?" Jack asked.

George shook his head. "I'm not sure, unless he intended to provide a key and never got around to it, or he sent it to Tom for safekeeping but planned to be the one to read it at some point in the future. I suppose he might have intended to give me the key to decode the document when we met on Saturday. Bosley was a good friend and an excellent writer, but he had a paranoid streak. Everything he's ever shared with me of any import has either been delivered personally or encoded with a key. The good news is, I knew him long enough that I'm fairly sure I can figure out how to read the notes he sent to Tom."

"Did you make a copy?" I asked.

"I brought the envelope here with me. Tom was intrigued by the idea of a mystery, but after what happened to Bosley, he decided he wanted to stay well out of whatever was going on."

I supposed I didn't blame him for that. "So, have you been able to make out any of it?" I asked.

"I haven't had the time yet. I do know the file refers to something called SIRP. All caps. I think it must be an acronym. I should have more when I can spend some time with Bosley's notes."

Jack frowned. "That seems familiar."

"SIRP sounds familiar to you?" Rick questioned.

"I don't remember where, but I feel as if I've seen it. It'll come to me."

Our conversation stalled as Meg offered everyone a refill on the tea. I took advantage of the lull to take a look around at her decorations. In the center of the museum was a miniature rendering of the town of Gull Island: The little shops, as well as the park and the marina, had been created via miniature houses, boats, and props. There were even little benches along the main drag, as well as tiny people. As she did every holiday, Meg had decorated the little town. Because it was October, she'd removed the baskets with brightly colored flowers from the busy downtown street and replaced them with pumpkins and apple carts. The minicarnival in the park had been replaced with a gazebo filled with jack-o'-lanterns, and the wharf, which jutted out into the marina, had orange lights strung along the railing that flashed on and off.

It really was charming. It made me warm and happy and kind of sad all at the same time.

"Any news about Billy's accident?" I asked, a feeling of melancholy beginning to take over.

Rick frowned. "I have news, but none of it's good."

I sat down in the chair I'd vacated and waited for him to go on.

"Okay, what exactly do you know?" Jack asked.

"Based on the damage to the vehicle, it appears Billy was hit from behind and run off the road. We're assuming, from the autopsy report and physical evidence found at the scene, that he hit his head in the crash. We don't know whether the blow to the head knocked him out, but it didn't kill him."

"What did kill him, then?" I asked.

"A gunshot to the chest."

Jack and I looked at each other.

"He was shot?" Jack asked.

Rick nodded. "It appears he landed on the beach when he was run off the road. The driver's side door was opened, and he was shot. The door was closed, and his car was pushed into the surf. The waves were pounding the coast last night, so if you hadn't come along when you did, there's a good chance the car would have been swept out to sea."

"So Billy was definitely murdered," I said.

"He was," Rick confirmed. "I assume, because he was still wearing his seat belt and there were no defensive wounds or evidence of any sort that he tried to get out of the car, Billy was knocked out in the crash. He was most likely unconscious when he was shot."

"I don't suppose you have a suspect?"

"Not at this point," Rick answered my question.

"Do you think Billy's death is related to Bosley's?" George asked the question Jack and I had been asking ourselves on the ride over.

Rick shrugged. "I don't know. I wish I did, but I don't. At this point, all we can do is investigate both deaths to see if they intersect."

Meg looked at Rick. "Bosley and Billy didn't know each other as far as I know, and now both men have been murdered. What can be going on?"

Rick looked at Meg with fatigue in his eyes. "I don't have a good feeling about any of this."

"Did your interviews turn up anything?" I wondered.

"I managed to eliminate a couple of people on the list. Trout Kellerman told me that Bosley had spoken to him shortly after he arrived on the island, wanting to know about people who'd lived here around the turn of the twentieth century, as well as any stories he might know involving the lighthouse, the hurricane that wiped out Skull Island, and the lighthouse keepers who lived there from 1893 to 1924. Trout told Bosley he wasn't the sort to be in to history or any sort of book learning, but he thought Sam Castle or Zane Carson might be able to help him."

"Did you believe him?" I asked Rick.

"I've known Trout a long time and have no reason to believe he would torture or kill a man. And he was a marginal student in school, so it fits that he wouldn't know much about the history of this area."

I glanced at Jack. He shrugged.

"Who else did you speak to?" I asked.

"I called Sam Castle and tried to speak to him, but he had a campaign dinner to prepare for. Zane Carson was out of town when I called, so I decided to try to speak to the two other fishermen on my list. It seemed like opportune timing because the storm had rolled in and it was unlikely they were out to sea. Buck Johnston was at the bar, drinking with his buddies, and mentioned he'd just returned from a weeklong charter that was cut short by two days by the storm. I figured if he'd been at sea for five days, he would have been away on both Friday and Saturday. I confirmed that with a couple of the other men who were part of the charter and were pouring down a cold one in the bar as well. That left Tizzy Tizdale. It took me several calls to find out he'd headed to Mexico a few weeks ago."

I took a breath and let it out. "Okay. So where does that leave us?"

"I still have about ten people on my list, including Sam Castle, Ron Remand, and Zane Carson," Rick said. "I'm hoping George can decipher the notes Bosley sent to Tom. I have a few other ideas I'm going to follow up on as well. Did the two of you find anything at the church yesterday?"

I let Jack explain the ledger he found and the high incidence of deaths on a single date. Meg still hadn't found anything that would explain the unusual occurrence, but she promised to keep looking. Jack and I wanted to go back to the church, and we needed to stop by the market, so I invited everyone to dinner that night, when we could further discuss the situation, and we left the museum. The rain had begun to let up, and this time I hoped it would stick.

We'd called ahead to let Pastor Branderman know we planned to come by again. He'd gone home early because of the rain but said we were welcome to come to his house to pick up the keys to the church and the basement if we promised to lock up and return them when we were finished. Jack agreed, so we headed there.

"What if November 12, 1924, is just a placeholder of some sort? What if it isn't an actual date of death after all?" I asked.

Jack frowned. "What do you mean?"

"I'm not sure exactly. The date is close to the end of the range of dates in the book. What if on November 12, someone went through the book and found a bunch of entries that had been overlooked but wanted to close out the log by making sure there was an entry for everyone who had died? Maybe they didn't want to take the time to research the actual death dates, so they entered that date to indicate each person had died before the ledger's end date."

Jack raised a brow. "I guess that's possible. I wonder how we can check."

"We'd need to verify the actual date of death for one or more of the people whose date of death is November 12, 1924, in the ledger. If we can find proof that a couple of them at least died on different dates, my placeholder theory begins to make sense."

"Okay. We'll make a list of names and try to track them down tomorrow."

We chatted with Pastor Branderman for a few minutes when we arrived at his house, then drove to the church. With dinner guests expected and our stop at the market, we were on a tight schedule, and I almost suggested we leave the visit to the church for the following day. But Jack wanted to make the list of people who had died on November 12, 1924, according to the ledger, and I wanted to look for a reference to SIRP. The more I thought about it, the more I agreed with Jack; the acronym did sound familiar.

"Okay, one hour and we're out of here," I said as we let ourselves in. "We can always come back another time if we still haven't found what we're looking for."

"All right," Jack said. "I'm going to grab the ledger I was looking at yesterday and start making a list of the people with a date of death of November 12, 1924."

"I'll go back through the files I was looking at yesterday. I know I saw SIRP somewhere."

Less than a minute later, I heard Jack swear.

"What is it?" I asked.

Jack handed me the ledger. "Look at the third name down on this page."

"Frederick Bowlington. Born January 31, 1875, and moved to the island, or at least the area this ledger covers, on April 12, 1895." I looked up at Jack. "Next to his name it says SIRP."

Jack nodded. "There's more. Look at the date of death."

"November 12, 1924."

******

One of the things I loved most about spaghetti was the smell of the sauce while it simmered. Back at the resort, Clara helped me make it, while Jack took Kizzy out for a romp and Garrett and George sat at the kitchen table, talking. Meg was coming over when the museum closed for the day, and Vikki had promised to be here as soon as she'd finished the chapter she was working on for her editor. Rick would join us if he could, but he did have two murders to solve, so he couldn't promise anything.

"I love the little display you made for the kitchen table," I said to Clara, who had arranged flowers, brightly colored leaves, and gourds from the farmers market. "I might do something similar for the dining table."

"I wanted to contribute," Clara answered. "Jack said he planned to bring over big pumpkins to carve for the front porch. I thought we could put one on the fireplace mantel as well."

"Speaking of Jack, I wanted to let you know we're entering into an experiment over the next two weeks. I'm going to be staying at his place, although I still plan to host the Halloween dinner here, and I'm sure I'll be popping in for coffee."

"Jack mentioned the cohabitation agreement you've come up with. Seems sort of formal and a bit silly to have to, the way you've been spending the night over there all the time anyway, but I support whatever the two of you want to do."

I guess it *was* sort of silly. I was almost forty years old. You'd think I'd have outgrown silly, but apparently, I hadn't. "If you or Garrett need anything, you just call. I'll be right down the path and can be here in less than a minute if need be."

"We'll be fine," Clara assured me. "I guess you've noticed Garrett and I have been spending a lot of time together since he moved back into the house."

"I had noticed."

Clara began chopping olives. "I think he might be the soul mate I foresaw when I first came here. We've talked about that—on more than one occasion, actually—and he says he feels the same way. At first, he wasn't open to the idea of a relationship. He said he didn't want me to be stuck with someone in a wheelchair. Not that I minded the chair, but he seemed to. But time passed, and he started doing better, and I think it might be time for us to take our relationship to the next level. I guess the only question is how you feel about us being together."

I smiled and placed my hand on her arm. "I feel fine about it. In fact, I'm better than fine. The two of you always seem so happy when you're together."

Clara reached for the garlic. "Okay, then. Now that we have that settled, let's gather some greens for the salad."

Maybe Jack was on to something when he asked me to move in with him. Given the way things were with Garrett and Clara, I was beginning to feel like a third wheel in the house. Oh, I knew I'd always be welcome here, as all the writers were, but it would be nice to give Garrett and Clara their space for at least part of the time. This was something I'd definitely have to think about.

Everyone had arrived by the time Clara and I had dinner ready. We all served ourselves, then gathered around the large dining table. One of the things I loved most about our group was when we ate dinner together, sharing the things that had happened during the day.

"Did you find what you were looking for in the church?" Rick asked.

"Yes," Jack replied, "at least part of it. If you remember, I mentioned there were a lot of entries where November 12, 1924, was recorded as the date of death. We went back to look and realized that next to the name of everyone who'd died on that date were the letters SIRP."

"Really?" Rick sounded amazed by that bit of information. "Any idea what SIRP stands for?"

Jack shook his head. "Unfortunately, we couldn't find a key or explanation. My best guess is that Bosley stumbled onto the dates and designation and researched it further. We're hoping whatever he sent to his friend Tom will help us figure out what he was on to."

"I plan to spend time on it later this evening," George said in response.

"I wonder if it would do any good to pick out a few names to research independently," Meg said. "If we started with the individual, then looked for birth, death, and whatever other records we could find, we'd at least be building a profile. If we could do that with several people, we might stumble over a link of some sort to SIRP."

"Do you think there are records going back that far?" Vikki asked.

"Sure," Meg answered. "Things like births, deaths, marriages, and such have been kept by churches for centuries. In terms of government records, not as long, but I'm sure we can find something if we look hard enough."

"I'll help you look if you show me what to do."

"Thank you, Vikki," Meg said. "I'd welcome the help."

"So, do you have news on either murder?" I asked Rick.

"I've continued to narrow down the suspect list, mainly by speaking to people and gathering alibis. So far, no one left on the list stands out over anyone else, so we'll just have to keep chipping away at it. I have the alleged arsonist to worry about as well."

"You're a busy man, with two murders and three fires to investigate," I said.

"Which is why I'm glad I can count on you to help out. It seems we all have things we're going to take responsibility for looking in to. Maybe we should meet here again tomorrow night," Rick suggested. "I'll bring pizza so no one has to cook."

We made sure everyone understood their assignments before we moved on to pie and coffee. This gave me a chance to bring up the Halloween dinner, which everyone seemed to be in to. I wanted to ask Gertie and her guy friend, Quinten, too, and even suggested that Rick might try enlisting him if he needed additional help. Quinten was not only a retired coroner, with a lot more experience investigating suspicious and violent deaths than any of us, he was ex-military, and he was a really good guy to boot.

I was pretty tired by the time the gathering wound down, so instead of packing clothes for two weeks, I just did it for one night. I'd get the remainder of my things the following day, when I was here to make a list of what I'd need to finish decorating the house.

"You have a minute?" Vikki poked her head in the door of my bedroom.

"Sure. Come on in. I'm just grabbing some clothes to take to Jack's."

"Clara told me about the cohabitation experiment. I want you to know I'm pulling for a successful trial."

I grinned. "Thanks. I wasn't sure about it when Jack first asked me to move in with him, thus the trial, but the more I think about it, the more certain I am."

"I'm really happy for you."

I paused and glanced at Vikki, who looked as if she had more on her mind than my tryout with Jack. "Something else you want to talk about?" I asked.

"I noticed the two guys from New Jersey in the two-bedroom cabin over by the marsh have left."

I nodded. "That's right. They left last week."

"I'd like to move over to that cabin if you haven't promised it to anyone."

I leaned a hip against the bedpost. "Okay. It isn't promised. Is the one-bedroom turning out to be too small?"

"Rick and I have been talking about moving in together. I want him to move out here, but he has a two-bedroom in town, and he needs space for a home office. I figured if one of the two-bedroom cabins was open, that would take away his argument for my moving into his place."

"Wow. Of course it's yours if you want it." I took a deep breath. "Wow again. This is huge."

"You seem more surprised by this than you were to have Jack ask you to move in with him."

"I guess I am. I shouldn't be, though. You never used to be the sort to want to settle down, but, of course, things have changed since Rick." I crossed the room and hugged Vikki. "I'm very happy for you both. I mean it. I think this is great. And I'll cancel the ad I was going to run next week for the two-bedroom. As far as I'm concerned, it's yours."

"Thanks, Jill. I'm not sure how this will work out, but I'm excited to try. I know Rick would like for us to get married. He's brought it up several times. I wasn't sure I was ready, but the truth is, time is running out. Rick would like to have children, and I'm beginning to realize I'd like it too. I'm looking at forty just around the corner, so if I want to have a family, it has to be now. Even with the lure of a baby, though, I find I'm hesitant. So, while it isn't as formally stated as what you and Jack have arranged, maybe moving in together is just the experiment Rick and I need to bring us to the point where any doubts we have are put to rest."

Chapter 5

Friday, October 26

I loved the way Gull Island went all-out for pretty much every holiday and special event. As a child, growing up in the shadow of my famous mother, I was never really afforded the opportunity to do kid stuff like carnivals, haunted houses, or trick-or-treating. Instead, I was dragged along to cocktail parties and boring dinner parties, where I would spend most of the evening trying to stay out of the way of the adults who'd come out to celebrate whatever trendy thing was making the rounds on the Hollywood social scene.

After I left home, I'd been so focused on building my career that I mostly let things like holidays and the hoopla associated with them go over and around me without paying much attention. Now, living on Gull Island and becoming part of both a family and a community for what felt like the first time, I found I rather liked the hoopla that came with coming together to celebrate whatever was cued up as the special event for each month's fund-raiser.

"Looks like a good turnout," Jack said as a pair of young boys dressed as Jedi stormtroopers plowed into us.

"The place is packed," I agreed. "Thankfully, the weather has cooperated."

Jack took my hand as he led me through the throngs of festival visitors around the wharf, where the haunted house and several food vendors had been set up.

"Did Brooke say where we should check in?" Jack asked.

"No, but it looks like there are a few other volunteers mingling around the ticket booth. Let's start there."

I took a deep breath as we walked along the wooden planks. The scent of kettle corn mingled with the charcoal smoke generated by the hot-dog vendor. My personal favorite festival snack was the garlic fries, but the tables filled with gooey caramel and bright-red candy apples had my mouth watering as well.

"Is Brooke around?" I asked the woman who was manning the ticket booth.

"She's inside. There's a door around the side for volunteers."

I looked toward the large building, which had been decorated to look like Dracula's castle. That wouldn't open for another half hour, yet already the line extended beyond the edge of the wharf and into the street. I had a feeling this was going to be a busy and profitable night.

Jack and I chatted with the woman about the crowds and nice weather for a few minutes, then headed to the side door. Inside, we found Brooke holding a clipboard in one hand and a cell phone in the other. She was talking on the phone but motioned for us to wait.

The windows had all been blacked out, so even with dim overhead lights the place was dark.

"Thank you both for coming," Brooke said, swiping a strand of blond hair away from her face. "I've had two of my actors call in sick." Brooke looked at Jack. "I don't suppose you'd mind playing a zombie?"

"Whatever you need me to do."

"Great." Brooke smiled. "Just follow that hallway to the last door on the left. My makeup crew will get you ready, then tell you what to do."

Jack gave me a quick kiss and promised to find me later.

Brooke turned her attention to me. "Jill, I need you on crowd control. There are four very distinct stages to this experience. Stage one is the outdoor part, which includes the tour of the haunted graveyard. Guests are then invited into the large room at the front of the building, where one of our actors tells the tale of the haunted castle and the people who once lived here. Once the intro is over, the interior doors open and the guests are led to the hallway where the real tour begins. That's stage three. After they make their way through the haunted hallways, they come out at the back of the building. There, they find the final stage, which includes a dark walk along the water, where we've set up lights and different optical illusions."

"Sounds like a huge undertaking," I commented.

"Oh, it was a bear to set up, but I think it's going to be awesome. I may end up moving you at some point, but for now I need you to work the entry room. You'll open the door that divides the exterior from the story room. You can fit up to a maximum of thirty people in that room. Once they've all filed in, you need to close the door, which is equipped with a one-way lock, so no one can sneak in. The narrator will come in and tell the tale, then you open the back door leading into the haunted hallway. As soon as everyone is out of the room, you close the back door, then go to the front one to let in the next group."

"Seems pretty straightforward."

"It is. We have it set up a lot like the Haunted Mansion at Walt Disney World. I have to warn you, though, there will be those who'll try to shove their way in even after the room is full. That's where you'll have to be assertive and make them wait. Thirty is the max. If you have twenty-nine and the next guests are a group of two, they wait."

"Got it."

"Good luck, and if you have any real problems, call me and I'll send backup."

"Don't worry. I should be fine," I said.

"Great." Brooke squeezed my arm. "And thanks again."

She hurried off to deal with something else within the interior of the large building, and I headed to the entry room with the two doors she'd described. I opened the room leading from the story room into the haunted hallway, which was just as I expected. Then I opened the door separating the front room from the line and was almost trampled to death.

"Wait," I yelled as I put my body between the room and the line. "We aren't open for another twenty minutes. I was just checking access."

There was a lot of grumbling, but the few people who had pushed past me went back out to the line to wait for the clock to work its way around to five.

"Yikes," I said when I had the room to myself again. I wondered if I shouldn't have borrowed a helmet and pads from the football coach at the high school. The crowd was terrifying.

Fortunately, once the event opened and the line started to move, things calmed down. It must have been interesting to walk through the graveyard, which had given those toward the front of the line something to keep them busy while they waited for the door to the story room to open. After two hours, another volunteer came by to trade with me: She'd take over as door monitor if I wanted to go back to the ticket booth. That sounded fine with me. The ticket booth was outside, near the water. After two hours of listening to the same three-minute story, I was ready for some fresh air and a change of scenery.

"I'm here to relieve you," I said to the woman who was manning the booth.

"Oh, good. I could use a change. The prices for each type of ticket are listed on the wall. Most people are buying tickets for the haunted house, but there are a few kiddie games along the boardwalk leading to the wharf, so we're selling tickets for those as well. The haunted house closes at nine, so you might want to cut off selling tickets at eight thirty. Unless, of course, the crowd dissipates between now and then, in which case use your best judgment."

"It sounds easy enough," I said as I took in the scent from the food vendors nearby. I was starving. I should have eaten something before we came out to the wharf.

The festival was in full swing by now, so there weren't many people who needed tickets. In fact, the long line we'd seen when Jack and I first arrived was gone, giving me time to people watch, which was always interesting at events like this. The kids running around with smiles of pure joy on their faces was probably the best part. Some wore costumes, others didn't, but they all looked to be having the best time. Groups of teens loitered in the area, while young couples with small children were steering them to the kiddie games.

The only thing that caused me to frown was a tall man in a skeleton costume. He had to be at least six-four, and his body as well as his head and face were completely covered by black material outlined in white. I watched him as he strode over to the rear of the haunted house, where the pathway leading from the building hugged the railing. He wasn't doing anything alarming exactly, but the way he stood, as if scanning the crowd while his face was completely concealed, left me feeling uncomfortable. Besides, there were signs posted informing spectators they couldn't loiter in the area because they needed to keep the exit clear.

I didn't suppose it was my job to play security guard. There were men mingling with the crowds wearing badges and carrying flashlights doing that. Yet I couldn't ignore the presence of the man either, and as far as I could tell there wasn't a single security guard in sight at that moment. Finally, I decided to walk over and speak to him. Maybe I'd recognize his voice, although I was pretty sure I didn't know anyone quite that tall.

Keeping my eye on the ticket booth, I trotted over to where he was standing. "Hello," I said. "My name is Jill. I'm a volunteer. I'm afraid we can't allow anyone to stand in the path of the exit. It's a safety issue. I hope you understand."

"I'm just waiting."

The man's voice was deep and unfamiliar. I was sure we'd never met.

"I completely understand. A lot of parents choose to wait for their children out here. There's a seating section right over there." I pointed. "Perhaps you can meet whoever you're waiting for there."

I couldn't see his face, but for some reason I pictured him snarling. "Thanks, but I think I'll just wait here."

A group of teens walked up to the ticket booth. I knew I should get back, but I hesitated. "I'm sorry, sir, but I'm going to have to ask you to move away from this walkway. As I said, it's a safety issue."

The man ignored me, which really made me angry. I was on the verge of using strong language to make my point when I turned around to glance at the ticket booth. One of the teenagers who'd been loitering in the area had opened the door to the booth and was about to step inside. "Oh, geez." I ran back toward my post. The last thing I needed was for the tickets as well as the income from the evening to go missing on my watch. By the time I shooed the kids off, the man in the skeleton suit was gone. I was glad he was no longer blocking the exit, but an instinctive fear remained in my chest.

The rest of the evening was uneventful, but I was relieved when Brooke showed up to collect my cash box and unused tickets.

"How'd it go?" she asked as she gathered everything together.

"It went well, except when I opened the door to the story room in the haunted house before we were ready and almost got trampled to death, and I had a small confrontation with a tall man dressed as a skeleton who refused to move away from the exit lane you set up from the rear of the cannery."

Brooke frowned. "You're the third person to tell me about the man in the skeleton costume. I'll be sure security knows to watch out for him if he shows up tomorrow. It always makes me nervous when adults dress up for these events. Especially adults who wear costumes that conceal their identities."

"Maybe you should ban costumes for people over a certain age next year," I suggested.

"It's been brought up in the past, but we don't have a lot of security, and what we do have is usually retired men who've offered to pitch in. That makes it hard to enforce a lot of rules."

I looked out at the throngs of people who were starting to head to the parking area. "Yeah, there are a lot of bodies to keep track of. I wonder if it might be worth it to hire a security company in the future."

"So far we haven't had any real problems, but if that changes, we might have to look in to something like that. This is a fund-raiser, though, and a private security company would be expensive. Especially with the festival so spread out. We have events here at the wharf and others by the museum and in the park in town."

"I guess it would be easier to provide security if everything was in a single location. Of course, that would make parking an issue. It looks like the last group in line for the haunted house just went in. I think I'll sneak in the back to wait for Jack."

Brooke put her hand on my arm. "Before you go, I have something to tell you that may help you with your research into Skull Island."

"Oh? What's that?"

She closed the door of the little ticket booth so we had a bit of privacy. "I'm not sure if you know her, but Sam Castle has a sister, Viv. She's married, so her last name is Marsh. Anyway, I ran into her earlier and we got to chatting, and I mentioned that a man who'd been researching the island had been murdered, and apparently, her grandfather told her a lot of really bad stuff happened on the island over the years. I asked about the couple of decades around the turn of the twentieth century, which I understand your writer friend was interested in, and she said that after the hurricane in 1893, the island became all but deserted until some guy brought a bunch of people there to do experiments on them."

"Experiments?"

"Viv admitted she didn't know all the details, but some scientist was doing tests on individuals who displayed symptoms of schizophrenia and other mental health issues. She said he brought them to Skull Island and used them as lab rats. It was all done in secrecy, so not a lot of people even know about it, but Viv thought some pretty awful things were done to those people in the name of science. It's one of those long-held family secrets no one is supposed to talk about, but she didn't see the harm in sharing it with me because it seemed to her if someone had proof of what was done to those poor people, it might be a reason to want that person dead."

******

After Jack was done with his zombie duties, we headed to his cabin and scrambled up some eggs rather than going out to eat with zombie makeup all over his face. I picked up Kizzy from the main house, where Garrett and Clara had been babysitting while Jack hopped into the shower.

The idea that mentally disabled individuals had been used as lab rats was disturbing, but despite Brooke's assertion that knowledge of what had happened to them could be a good motive for murder, I wasn't sure how it could lead to two men being killed a century later. Chances were the story Brooke had heard had nothing to do with either Bosley or Billy's deaths, but Jack felt there was enough there to warrant further research, so we were going to have something quick to eat and then settle down at our computers to see what we could dig up.

"So, how was the haunted cannery?" Garrett asked.

I bent down to greet Kizzy, who was doing the abandoned-dog happy dance at my feet. "I was working the entire time and didn't actually have a chance to walk through, but the wharf area was packed, and it looked as if everyone was having fun. Jack got to be a zombie, so he was able to see the interior of the haunted house; he said it was good and spooky this year. I think we might try to walk through it together tomorrow evening."

"I used to enjoy going to stuff like that, but I'm afraid at my age, and given my health, something mellower and less crowded is more my speed. I'm glad you had a good turnout. The town and the school can use the money."

"Brooke seemed to be happy with the attendance. She made the rounds to all the venues, and things were hopping pretty much everywhere."

"The town is lucky to have her," Clara said. "She goes out of her way to make sure that everything is organized and gets done."

I pulled up a chair and sat down for a minute. "Speaking of Brooke, she mentioned to me that Skull Island was used as an experimental facility for the mentally ill after the hurricane in 1893. I don't suppose you know anything about it?"

Garrett shook his head. "I don't remember hearing that. Not that it didn't occur. Information wasn't as readily available back then, and something like that sounds like the sort of thing the folks behind it might have wanted to keep quiet."

"I wonder how we can find out more about it."

"The library has old books and journals. Meg has a lot of original documents at the museum as well. Then, there are the notes Bosley left behind that George's still working on. I imagine if what Brooke told you was true, Bosley would have stumbled across it during the course of his research."

"Do you think finding proof of something like that could be what got Bosley killed?"

Garrett shrugged. "Whatever went on happened a long time ago. I don't see how anyone living today would be affected."

I rubbed the back of my neck as I tried to work through things in my mind. "I guess you're right, but it seems to me that given the timing of things, they seem more than just a little coincidental."

"It does seem whatever Bosley was on to took place on that island between 1893 and 1924. If people were detained illegally and sent to the island to be used in experiments, I guess it's possible it might affect reputations even today. If nothing else, it's worth looking in to."

Chapter 6

Saturday, October 27

Jack and I had worked for several hours the night before but were unsuccessful in finding any information on the lab experiments that might have taken place on the island. If people were brought there, as Viv had indicated, there didn't seem to be a record of it. At least not one that was available on the internet.

We both had volunteer duty this morning, so we dropped Kizzy off with Garrett and Clara again and went into town. I hoped to find time to chat with George today to see if he had anything to report on Bosley's notes, and I also wanted to track Rick down because he must have been working on both murders.

First, though, Jack and I had a kiddie carnival to survive. Last year, we'd been stationed at the dart booth, which attracted older kids and teens who had been, generally speaking, mean. I hoped we'd get a different assignment. I supposed adults who had more practice dealing with adolescents might have done better.

"Oh, good, just in time," Brooke greeted us. "Jack, I need you over on the rope climb, and Jill, I hoped you wouldn't mind doing the fishing booth."

I looked around. I didn't see any water. "Fishing booth?"

Jill handed me several poles with ropes tied to clothesline clips. "The game's meant for the younger kids; usually, those between three and seven. When you get to your booth, you'll find a blanket with a bunch of little toys behind it. When one of the kids tosses their line over the blanket, you clip on a toy. It's a little boring but really easy, and the little kids are usually dressed up so cute."

"That sounds perfect for me," I said. "Where do I go?"

"Down the second row of booths to the very end. There'll be another volunteer there to work with you. One of you can run the front, taking the tickets and helping the kids cast their lines, and the other can clip on the prizes."

Jack and I said our goodbyes and went our separate ways. There were a lot of people out and about on this lovely autumn morning, although not nearly as many as there'd been at the haunted house the previous evening. The Saturday morning crowd tended to consist of parents with their younger children for nonscary Halloween fun. The kiddie carnival was near the museum, and I knew it would be open today and was hosting a Halloween storytime for the little ones.

"You must be Jill," a cheery woman with short blond hair, brown eyes, and a sunny smile said when I arrived. "I'm Jessica Carson."

"I'm happy to meet you, Jessica. I don't suppose you're related to Zane Carson?"

"I'm his younger sister. Much younger. We share a father but have different mothers."

"So, your father is Zachary Carson, who's descended from Isaak Carson, one of the founding fathers."

The plump woman clapped her hands. "It looks like someone has been doing her homework."

"I work with Jack Jones at the newspaper, and we've been looking into the history of the island for some of the articles we're working on. I find it interesting that everyone knows about and talks about the ancestry of Zane Carson, Sam Castle, Billy Waller, and Ron Remand, but no one really talks about their siblings. Why is that?"

Jessica laughed. "The founding fathers were chauvinists for sure. All four men had multiple children, but it was the oldest son in each of the families who got the recognition, and the power that came with a seat on the island council."

"So the original island council was a committee of founding fathers?"

Jessica nodded. "Yes, and at that time the council was so much more than it is now. In the beginning, it was the law on the island, and the council members were basically kings of their own little kingdoms. It was a big deal to be the eldest son because he would someday inherit his father's seat on the council."

"So everyone has had a son to pass the torch to?"

"So far. I don't begrudge Zane the prestige that comes with being the eldest son. By now, it doesn't mean a lot anyway. Over time, as the island grew, the people who moved here wanted more representation, so seats were added, diluting the power of the eldest sons."

I began arranging the fishing poles for the kids who would be arriving soon. "I understand Zane is really in to the historical aspect of things."

"He is. He knows a lot about history and feels it's important to preserve the vision the founding fathers left us, despite the evolution of the population on the island. Zane's a serious guy with serious ideas. He would have been happier had he lived a few generations ago. Me, I'm all for growth and change. I think a community that grows stagnant is a community that dies."

"I guess you heard about what happened to Billy Waller?"

Jessica frowned. "I did hear. I can't imagine who would want to kill Billy. He was the nicest guy you'd ever want to meet. He never let the whole founding father thing go to his head the way some of the others did. He cared about the island and the people on it. He was such a pure soul. Killing him makes no sense."

"There's an idea floating around that Billy and one of our writers, Bosley Newman, were killed because of something they knew. Do you have any idea what that might be?"

Jessica furrowed her brow. "*They* might know. You think the same person killed both men? Did they know each other?"

"Bosley was a writer of historical novels. He was on the island to do research on the Skull Island lighthouse. We know from his notes that he spoke to a lot of people who would have been living on the island for a long time, including Billy, Zane, Sam, and Ron."

Jessica paused. I saw a look of awareness cross her face a split second before she changed the subject. "It looks like the kids have just been let in through the front gate. Do you want to run the front or the back?"

"I'll start in the back, then we can trade after an hour or so."

I wished I'd had more time to grill Jessica, but the kids were indeed running in our direction. I could sense she knew something. What I didn't know was why, if she cared about Billy, as she seemed to, she'd clam up about whatever it was she knew if it could help us find his killer. I hoped there would be a lull in the action at some point so I could talk to her again, but it was Saturday, and it was a gorgeous day, so there was a steady crowd until Jessica's relief came so she could head over to the haunted house.

By the time Jack and I were released from our volunteer duties, the entire town was packed. Jack had picked up a lead during his stint with the rope climb about Billy's death that seemed like a long shot, and we thought about following it as far as it went; you never knew where a clue, even a weak one, might lead. Ultimately, we decided to track down Rick and share it with him instead. I was fairly certain he'd be out on patrol with the town filled to capacity, so I texted him to ask if he had time to meet us somewhere for a quick chat. He texted back that he was heading to the food court for a pulled pork sandwich, so we went in that direction as well.

Rick already had a table and a sandwich when we arrived, so we sat down to talk while he ate.

"So, what's this lead you have?" Rick asked as he washed down his sandwich with a soda.

Jack answered. "During my stint at the kiddie carnival, I spoke with a man who asked to remain anonymous."

"Figures," Rick grumbled. "Okay, what did this anonymous man have to say?"

"That Billy Waller was seen in town having dinner with a man he used to own some investment property with on the night he died."

"You have my interest," Rick said. "Does *this* man have a name?"

"Vincent O'Brian. At one point they'd pooled their money and bought a couple of duplexes as well as an apartment building. The investment properties were a problem from day one, and in the end, they both lost a lot of money. They sold the properties at a huge loss. Billy remained on the island and went on to other things, while Vincent moved to Charleston and started a property management company."

"You learned all this while you were manning the climbing ropes?" Rick asked.

"I'm a reporter. I'm naturally inquisitive."

"Okay." Rick wiped his mouth with his napkin. "Go on."

"My source happened to be dining in the same restaurant as Billy and Vincent. They appeared to be engaged in a serious conversation. There wasn't any yelling going on, or anything that screamed *disagreement*, but the expressions on their faces were very intense. My source wanted to make it clear he wasn't necessarily accusing Vincent of anything; he just thought it was curious that a man who'd once partnered up with Billy happened to be having dinner with him less than an hour before he died."

"And how did your source know when Billy died?" Rick asked.

Jack shrugged. "I might have mentioned the approximate time I found Billy's car in the water."

Rick popped the last bite of his sandwich into his mouth, chewed, and swallowed. "Okay. I know Vincent, so I'll track him down to see if he has anything to say about his dinner with Billy. Anything else?"

"Not at the present time," Jack answered.

"How about you?" I asked Rick as he balled up his napkin and tossed it into the trash. "Do you have any news for us?"

Rick picked up his soda cup and shook the ice. "On Billy's death, no. On the house fires, yes."

"You know who set them?" I asked.

Rick nodded. "It turns out it was a bunch of teens undergoing initiation for a street gang on the island."

I frowned. "I'd pretty much guessed it would be kids, but a street gang? I didn't know we had any here."

"We don't. Or at least we didn't until recently. It seems one of the local boys—who's a minor, so I won't give his name—visited his cousin in Chicago over the summer. This cousin belongs to a gang there. The local boy, for reasons only a teen could come up with, decided being part of a gang would be cool— my word, not his; I'm sure kids don't say *cool* anymore, but I'm not up on the current lingo. When he returned to the island at the end of summer, he started his own gang. He gathered some other teens to organize, and they decided it was important to pledge their allegiance by committing some illegal act and chose house fires."

"I assume the parents of these misguided boys are on the hook for damages?" Jack asked.

"Damages and more. What started out as a foolish idea is going to create a whole lot of grief for everyone involved."

I had to admit I felt sorry for the parents, who might very well have their life savings wiped out. It was at times like this that I patted myself on the back for deciding children wouldn't be part of my life.

Rick left to do another sweep of the festival, and Jack and I went to get something for our own lunch. I settled on a hamburger, while Jack went for the steak sandwich.

"So what now?" I asked as we sat down to eat.

"We can go look for George," Jack suggested. "He said he'd be working on decoding the papers Bosley sent to Tom, and it seems as if finding out what Bosley wanted to protect is our best bet at discovering who killed him."

"I'll call him after we eat. I'm not sure if he planned to spend the day at his cabin or somewhere else." I glanced toward the haunted maze that had been set up using hay bales. "It would be fun to participate in a few of the attractions. I'd love to do the maze, and maybe the haunted house, although both would be better after dark."

"Let's look for George. Maybe spend some time with Kizzy; take her for a walk along the beach. Then plan to come back after dark for dinner and some good old-fashioned fun."

"Sounds like a plan." I grinned.

While the plan sounded good, it never actually came to fruition. Brit waved us down and joined us at our table just as we were finishing up.

"Are you here to volunteer?" I asked.

"I did this morning. It was fun, but I've definitely had enough kiddie time for one day. I was going to head home when I saw you sitting here and wanted to share my news."

"News?" I asked.

"I ran into a friend from my theater group who told me that Bosley rented a boat from her brother the day before he died."

"Who's the friend and who's her brother?" Jack asked.

"Michelle Franklin, and her brother's name is Logan. He works over at the marina. Anyway, Michelle just happened to be there, trying to get her brother to let her use his Mustang for a date she had that night when Bosley came in to ask about renting a boat. She waited while her brother took care of the paperwork. She didn't know where Bosley went or why he needed the boat, but she remembered he only rented it for a day."

"And she was sure it was Bosley? She knew who he was?" I asked.

"Not at the time. But after he died, and everyone was talking about it, she wondered, so she asked her brother if the guy who was found dead on the beach was the same person who'd rented the boat, and he said it was. I asked her if her brother had mentioned the boat rental to the cops, but she said he hadn't. No one asked him about it, and he wanted to stay out of it."

"Okay, thanks," I said. "I'll let Rick know."

"I wonder if the boat had GPS," Jack said. "A lot of rental boats do. It allows the agency to track them in case of theft or accident."

"Do you think the system might have a record of where Bosley went?" I asked.

"It wouldn't hurt to head over to the marina to find out."

I called Rick, who was swamped at the moment with the fallout from a street fight between two groups of out-of-town teens. He suggested Jack and I talk with Logan Franklin. If there seemed to be something there, he'd follow up with him when he was free.

The marina was an insanely busy place during the summer but provided a much more laid-back feel as the days shortened toward winter. It was a Saturday, however, and the weather was simply gorgeous today, so a lot of the slips that usually housed boats were empty. I hoped we'd find Logan in the rental office, and luckily, we did. Jack introduced us both and explained why we'd stopped by, then asked Logan if he could take short break to speak to us.

"I don't want to get pulled into whatever's going on," Logan said, a tone of hesitation evident in his voice.

"We just want to ask you a few questions," Jack reassured him. "If you can't take a break, we can ask them right here."

"You won't put my name in the paper?"

Jack shook his head. "I won't mention you by name at all. Right now, writing a story about what happened to Bosley Newman is very much secondary to figuring out what happened to him."

"He was a friend of a friend," I added.

Logan still looked uncertain, though he nodded. "Okay. But I don't know a lot. I was here on Thursday, arguing with my sister, when this old guy came in, wanting to rent a boat for the day. He had a wad of cash and was offering a good tip, so I didn't ask a lot of questions. He took the boat out at around ten in the morning and brought it back before the marina closed at five."

"Was he alone?" Jack asked.

"He was alone when he came in to rent the boat, but he mentioned he was picking someone up along the way. He wanted to be sure the boat was outfitted with two life jackets."

"Was he alone when he returned at the end of the day?"

"As far as I could tell. He was alone when he came in here to drop off the keys."

"Did he say where he was going?" I asked.

Logan shifted his eyes. "No, he didn't say."

"I feel like you know something you aren't telling us," I said.

"I spoke to a buddy of mine who was out fishing that day. When it came out that the guy's body washed up on the beach, I mentioned he rented a boat from me. My buddy said he recognized a boat he saw moored off Skull Island as one of mine. We both suspected it was the old guy out on the island that day."

"Do your boats have GPS?" Jack asked.

"Yeah, but only in real time; we don't log a history. The GPS is there just to keep an eye on them in case someone decides to steal one."

"Okay, thanks." Jack handed Logan one of his cards. "Call me if you hear or remember anything. We'd really like to figure out what happened to our friend."

From the marina we drove to the resort to pick up Kizzy at the main house and take her for a walk. I was sure she'd be ready for some exercise. Jack suggested we see if George was around after that. Maybe he'd have news that would move this mystery forward.

******

"I have found something," George said to us as we took chairs at his kitchen table with cups of hot coffee. "I don't know for certain that Bosley's theory led to his death, but if it's true, it's disturbing."

Jack leaned forward, resting his arms on the table in front of him. "Let's hear what you found, and we can figure out what to do with it after that."

George took a sip from his cup, then began. "I'm not sure how he found it, but it seems Bosley came across something relating to a man named Oswald Bollinger, a rich man by any standards. He was an heir to old money, but he was also a scientist who studied abnormal psychology during the late nineteenth century, which no one would argue was a dynamic time for the field. I don't want to bore you with all the details, but I'd like to offer a few points to give you a feel for what I mean by *dynamic*."

Jack and I both nodded for him to continue.

George began to read from his computer screen. "In 1883, the first experimental psychology research lab in the United States was opened at Johns Hopkins University. In 1886, the first textbook on psychology was published, the same year Sigmund Freud opened his practice in Austria. By the time the hurricane wiped out most of the population on Skull Island in 1893, psychology had really taken off. There were twenty experimental psychology research laboratories in this country alone."

George's voice seemed to rise in volume as he continued to discuss a field he obviously found fascinating.

"In 1896, a paper that basically gave birth to the idea of social behaviorism was published. Briefly, behavior, even deviant or socially inappropriate behavior, is learned, and thus can be modified. Bollinger tried to find his place in the rapidly growing field of behavioral psychology but never quite found his niche."

I had a feeling I could see where this was going, and it wasn't going to be good.

"When Bollinger couldn't find a way to make a name for himself working within the academic structure of the time, he came up with the idea of isolating a group of people who had demonstrated socially undesirable behavior and use his own methods, which he'd been developing for several years, to create change in them. From the notes Bosley found, Bollinger sought out the most highly disturbed: people who heard voices and experienced hallucinations on a regular basis."

"So, schizophrenics," Jack said.

"Among others. Bollinger needed a place to do his experiments, so he approached Gull Island's council members with a proposal that would grant him a large tract of land for a sizable amount of money. The men on the council at that time didn't want a group of seemingly dangerous men and women brought to Gull Island, but they were tempted by the money, so they worked out a deal with Bollinger to use the existing infrastructure on Skull Island, which was all but deserted by then."

"So they rounded these people up like cattle?" Jack asked.

"It seems they did. Bollinger looked for individuals who seemed to be on their own in the world, and who suffered from the disturbances he'd targeted. They were taken to Skull Island, where he conducted his experiments. If they were properly documented, it seems Bosley never found the records."

"This sounds awful, but how could it lead to Bosley's death?" I asked.

George held up a hand. "Hang on; I'm getting to that." He cleared his throat before continuing. "Bosley found the same mentions of all the deaths in 1924 Jack did, and he, like you, noticed the designation SIRP. It was Bosley's theory that the names of the men and women who were relocated to Skull Island were all given that designation, and that date of death. Despite his best efforts, he was never able to confirm that SIRP and Bollinger were related. His notes suggest the experiments went wrong and the project was shut down in 1924."

"What do you mean by shut down?" Jack asked.

"He thought the participants who remained on the island were exterminated," I realized.

"That was his theory, one he was trying to prove when he was murdered. It was also his theory that the men on the council at that time knew about everything that went on from the inception of the idea of the experiment to the extermination of the participants. Bosley thought those men were compensated financially in exchange for their silence."

Holy cow. It seemed Bosley certainly had stirred up a hornets' nest.

Chapter 7

As we'd planned, Jack and I went back into town for dinner and the festival after sunset. Walking around the crowded streets while adults and children alike lined up for events, munched on the goodies sold on almost every corner, and shopped in the mom-and-pop shops, which had stayed open late, was the best time I'd had in quite some time.

"The line for the haunted maze is really long and I understand there's a certain amount of running involved, so I think we should start there and then think about dinner," I suggested.

"Running?" Jack asked.

"From what I heard while I was at the fishing booth this morning, the maze has one correct path and a lot of fakes. If you wander onto a path that's a dead end, not only have you wasted your time but a ghost or ghoul may jump out from the shadows and chase you back to the correct route."

Jack laced his fingers through mine. "It sounds like fun. I'm glad you told me what to expect so I won't have a heart attack at the first wrong turn."

"The daytime maze is designed for little kids, but once it gets dark, terror is what the event organizers are going for."

"Why don't you get in line and I'll grab the tickets?" Jack suggested. "The line at the ticket booth is almost as long as the one for the maze. Double-teaming will save us time."

"Okay, but don't get distracted. I know how you like to gab when you run into people you know."

"No gabbing, I promise."

We parted, and Jack headed toward the ticket booth, while I went to the end of the line. If the line at the haunted house was as long as this one, it was going to take us the rest of the evening to check out just these two attractions. Not that I really minded. The kiddie games were pretty tame for adults, and the twirling and spinning rides the teens enjoyed made me nauseated. It was fun just to be here with Jack, enjoying the excitement generated whenever so many people came together with the explicit purpose of having fun.

"Hey, Jill. You here alone?" a woman I knew from the spin class I occasionally attended but whose name escaped me asked.

"No, I'm with Jack. He went to get the tickets. Are you on your own?"

The woman shook her long red ponytail. "I'm with Sissy Gardner, and like Jack, she went for the tickets. These lines are so long. The only way to see everything is to divide and conquer."

"It does seem there are a lot of people out tonight, which is good for the bottom line."

"Speaking of the bottom line, did you hear the cashbox for the haunted house was stolen?"

I raised a brow. "Stolen? Really? How did that happen?"

She leaned in just a bit. "I heard some tall guy in a skeleton costume was loitering around the exit of the haunted house, acting sort of mysterious, so the woman who was assigned to the ticket booth stepped away from it for just a minute to ask him to move on. He refused, and it took her longer than she anticipated to deal with him. While she was distracted, someone made off with the cash from the entire afternoon. I understand there were several thousand dollars in the box."

I remembered the man from the previous evening. I'd be willing to bet he was working with the boys who'd almost gotten away with the cash from last night's haul.

"Brooke is livid," the redhead continued. "Not at the volunteer; she was just doing what she thought was best. At the thieves who'd steal money from a school fund-raiser."

"Did anyone call Deputy Savage?" I asked.

She nodded. "Brooke did. He came to take a statement and will be keeping an eye out for the tall skeleton. In the meantime, Brooke's going to go around more often to collect the money from the ticket sales. She got busy this afternoon, so the cashbox had a good four hours' worth of receipts."

By the time Jack made his way back to me, Sissy had returned to the line as well. The four of us chatted for a few minutes before we turned around to face the front of the line. I filled him in on the theft, and he said the woman who sold him the maze tickets told him that Rick had a suspect in custody. I sure hoped he'd caught whoever had stolen the cash and the money had been recovered.

"I overheard some teenagers talking when I was on my way back to you who said the secret to making it through this thing is to make two rights for every left turn," Jack whispered.

"Oh, I wish you hadn't told me. It's no fun to try to figure it out if you have the trick to it."

"I understand there are a few surprises even for those who stay on the right path. I'm sure you'll get your money's worth of scream-worthy moments before we're done."

I hoped Jack was right, although at the rate the line was moving, we'd be doing good if we got to the front of the line before the maze closed for the evening. "Oh, look, there's Meg." I waved to her as she walked toward us.

"I'm glad I found you," she said.

"Is something wrong?" I asked. "George?"

"George is fine, but I do have something to tell you. I hate to ask you to get off the line, but I think my news is best shared in a less-crowded place."

I glanced at Jack. He nodded. "Okay," I said. "Let's find a place to talk."

We followed Meg through the crowd and to the far side of the big dirt lot that was being used for parking. "So what's up?" I asked.

"A friend of mine stopped by the museum just as I was locking up for the day. She'd heard what had happened to Bosley, who she'd met in the museum earlier in the week, when he came in to look through some journals. She told me that she might know something important, but after what happened to Bosley and Billy, she wasn't sure she wanted to get involved."

"Okay," I said as a car slowly drove by. "What did she say?"

"Lily lives across the street from Billy. On the Friday night the ME thinks Bosley was killed, he came to Billy's home at around five. She didn't recognize his car, but she happened to be in her yard turning on her Halloween lights when he pulled up. She remembered him as the man she'd met at the museum and didn't think anything of Bosley being there. She knew he was doing historical research, and Billy's family has lived on the island as long as anyone. It wasn't until she heard he'd been murdered that she began thinking about things."

I glanced back toward the carnival area, which was still as crowded as ever, then back at Meg. "So Bosley went to see Billy on the night he died, and then Billy ended up dead a couple of days later. The visit seems relevant. Did she say how long Bosley was there?"

"That's just it. She said he never left."

"He didn't leave Billy's house on Friday night?" Jack asked.

"Not that she saw," Meg said, then took a deep breath. "Let me back up a bit. Lily told me she saw Bosley arrive at around five. And she also saw Sam Castle arrive, she estimated sixty to ninety minutes later. She wasn't watching the time because she didn't think it was going to turn out to be important."

"Okay. Bosley shows up at Billy's, then Sam shows up. Then what?" I asked.

"Both their vehicles were in the drive for quite a while. When she looked outside later, as she was locking up for the night, she noticed Sam's vehicle was gone, but Bosley's was still there. It was gone when she looked outside the next morning."

"So maybe Billy killed Bosley," Jack said.

"Then who killed Billy?" I countered. "What if Billy, Bosley, and Sam all went somewhere in Sam's car? What if Bosley knew something that made the other men uncomfortable, so they took him somewhere and tried to get him to give up whatever proof he claimed to have? What if he wouldn't, so either Sam or Billy killed him, then dumped his body in the ocean? Sam lives on the coast and has a boat he moors at a private dock."

"Then a few days later," Jack continued where I left off, "after he had a chance to consider things, Billy decides he can't live with his guilt. He tells Sam he's going to turn himself in, but Sam doesn't want to spend the rest of his life in prison, so he follows Billy into town, where we know he had a dinner meeting, then runs him off the road and kills him."

"How do we prove any of this?" Meg asked.

No one spoke right away. Eventually, I said, "I wonder what happened to Bosley's car. Someone must have moved it late on Friday night."

"That's a really good question," Jack said. "I wonder if Rick has already looked into locating it."

"We need to ask him."

"He was over near the haunted house dealing with the theft when I last saw him," Meg offered.

"I'll text him to see if he has a minute to talk." I took out my phone and sent a quick message.

"If Sam Castle killed Bosley and Billy, we'll need irrefutable proof," Meg added. "He's rich and well connected. A loose theory based on circumstantial evidence is never going to fly."

Meg was right. If Sam was guilty, we were going to need solid evidence to prove it, which might not be easy to get.

I was just about to try calling Rick when he texted me back. He was on his way to his office to process the paperwork on the kids who'd stolen the money from the haunted house ticket booth, and we could meet him there.

******

The money from the ticket booth was stolen by four boys, all in their teens. Their parents had been notified and the boys had been slapped on the wrists, then turned over to them. Most of the money was still in the box, and the few dollars they'd spent at the food court had been covered by their parents before the boys were released.

Rick was waiting for Meg, Jack, and me in his office.

"What about the guy in the skeleton outfit?" I asked.

"The boys said he wasn't with them."

I frowned. "That doesn't seem right. He was the one who distracted me last night when the kids almost got away with the cashbox, and the volunteer tonight said she went to ask him to move away from the exit of the haunted house when the boys snuck in and made off with the cashbox. It seems he was the distraction."

Rick shrugged. "I thought so too, but I spoke to the four boys individually and they all insisted that while they took advantage of the distraction, he wasn't part of their plan."

"They might be lying," Jack said. "The guy might have recruited them in the first place, and coached them about what to say if they were caught."

"Jack's right," I said. "It makes sense there would be an adult behind the whole thing."

"Maybe," Rick agreed, "but I don't have a reason to bring him in at this point, even if I knew who he was or where to find him, which I don't. I plan to keep an eye out for him, though. Now, you said you had something about the two deaths?"

Jack took the lead in filling Rick in. I could see by the changing expressions on his face that he thought our theory was a possibility.

"It sounds like I need to have a chat with Sam Castle," Rick said.

"I'm not trying to tell you how to do your job, but wouldn't it be better to try to find some sort of proof first? If you let him know you're on to him before you have something on him, you'll just tip him off. He might even take off."

"I don't think so. He has too much to lose. If I had proof of his involvement I'd certainly gather it before I spoke to him, but right now all we really have is your theory."

"What about Bosley's car?" I asked. "Did you ever find it?"

"No."

"Maybe we should spend a few hours trying to track it down," I suggested. "It might be behind

Billy's house for all we know. Or at Sam's, although that would be dumb on Sam's part."

"If there's evidence to find and Sam is our killer, it's doubtful he left it anywhere we'd be likely to find it. I suppose he could have left it at Billy's if he wanted to make it look like Billy killed Bosley. I don't suppose it would hurt to head over there to take a look."

"I need to meet George," Meg said. "Call us and let us know what you find."

"Jack and I will go with you," I said to Rick. "We already lost our place in line at the maze. We might as well try for some other excitement tonight."

*****

Billy had lived on a quiet street where the lots were large, the homes larger, and tall trees lined the road. Rick pulled up alongside the curb and parked. The three of us got out.

Billy had once been married. He had three children, all grown, and had been living alone when he died. The house was dark, but Rick went up to the front door and knocked. He wanted to be sure to follow protocol just in case one or more of the children were currently in residence. While Rick went to the front door, Jack and I scooted around the back. I didn't see a vehicle of any type in the yard, and a quick peek through the window of the garage revealed that other than a motorcycle, the building was empty of vehicles of any type.

"Bosley's car isn't here," I said when we came back to the front door. "It could have been moved by now anyway."

117

"I wonder if it had an OnStar or something similar," Jack mused. "If so, you might be able to track it that way."

"I'll check," Rick said. "I need to get back to the festival. I got a call while you were around back that the teen gangs who've come to the island for the weekend are fighting again. I don't want anyone to get hurt. I'll have one of my men confirm Sam's whereabouts on the night Billy died. We know he was with him the night Bosley died, but if things played out the way we think, he won't have an alibi for Tuesday night. If you stumble across any new information text me; otherwise, we can talk again tomorrow."

Rick drove us back to the station, where we'd left Jack's truck. When Rick returned to the festival, we did so as well.

I thought our theory was a good one, but Rick was right: We had no proof things had happened the way we thought. Unless…

"If Sam Castle's boat was used to dump Bosley's body, there should be some physical evidence of it," I said. "Blood or something."

"Rick will need a warrant to search the boat."

"Rick will, but we won't. We know where it's docked. It would only take a few minutes to sneak aboard and take a peek around."

"The boat is docked at Sam's home," Jack reminded me. "He's sure to have a security system."

"For his home, but maybe not for his boat. Let's head to the marina. I have a plan."

My plan was to use Jack's boat to get to Sam's boat from the water. I had no doubt he would have a security system protecting his property, so accessing his dock from the road would probably never work, but I doubted whatever system he had would prevent the boat from being boarded from the water. We didn't have a key, of course, so we might not be able to get into the vessel's interior, but if Bosley's body had been dumped from the boat, there should be some evidence on the deck.

When we arrived at the marina, the parking lot was deserted except for a single vehicle, a white Ford F250. Jack pulled into a spot. He kept a key to his boat in the glovebox of his truck, so he hadn't needed to return to either of his homes to pick it up. I settled into the lounge, which had both an indoor and outdoor section that looked out toward the back of the vessel while he dealt with the prelaunch duties required each time the boat left the dock. Although a bit on the chilly side, it was a beautiful, starry evening. I couldn't help but think how romantic it would be to take a cruise under the stars that didn't involve murder and an ongoing investigation.

"Sam lives on the channel," Jack said as he pulled away from the dock and slowly began to make his way through the marina. "It'll take about fifteen minutes to get there when we reach open water. There's wine in the cupboard if you want to open a bottle and pour us both a glass. As long as we're out here on a beautiful night like this one, we may as well enjoy ourselves."

I walked across the boat to the cabinet where I knew he kept his alcohol. I picked out a hearty Zinfandel and opened it, then chose two large glasses. I poured some of the deep red liquid into each glass, recorked the bottle, then walked back to where he was sitting. After handing him one of the glasses, I put my free hand on his shoulder and leaned a hip against his seat.

"This is really nice. Why is it we don't do this more often?"

"I don't know," Jack answered. "We should plan a trip."

"How about tomorrow?"

Jack turned slightly and looked at me. "Tomorrow?"

"It occurred to me that it might be a good idea to go out to Skull Island and take a look around. Maybe there's some sort of evidence there we can use to pull this whole thing together. Even if there isn't, it's supposed to be a nice day. We can bring a picnic and Kizzy and make a day of it."

"Sure," Jack said. "I'm kind of over the Harvest Festival anyway."

I smiled. "Good. Then it's a date."

"Should we invite the others?" Jack asked. "Not that I wouldn't love to have a romantic day at sea with you, but George has already mentioned a trip to the island."

I took a sip of my wine and nodded. "I guess it would be appropriate to invite the whole group. I'll start a text right now to let them know what we're planning."

While I did that, Jack sailed on toward where Sam lived. Once he'd entered the channel, we needed to reduce our speed significantly, so it took another ten minutes to make our way to his property.

"The boat's gone," I said as Jack slowed even further as we approached Sam's house. "That seems strange to me."

"Maybe," Jack said. "Or maybe Sam's just out, or maybe the boat is in for repairs, or maybe, like many recreational boaters, he chose to dry-dock the vessel for the winter. It *is* late October."

"I suppose the boat's absence could be explained by any one of those reasons, but if you ask me, it's somewhere having all the blood cleaned off." I let out a breath. "Let's head back. George texted me to say he's at the main house with Meg, Garrett, and Clara. They all want to come with us to the island tomorrow. George suggested we stop by to talk with them this evening if we get back in time. I guess they've been busy working up some additional theories."

Chapter 8

Sunday, October 28

Last night's brainstorming session hadn't netted us any strong ideas about what might have occurred on the nights of Bosley and Billy's deaths, but given the fact that they were seen together the night Bosley died, we were still fairly certain they were connected in some way or another.

In his official capacity as deputy, Rick had done quite a bit better at tracking down real answers than Jack and I. He'd spoken to Sam and confirmed that he had been invited to Billy's that night to talk about the history of Skull Island and the lighthouse. When he left, he said, Billy and Bosley were still talking. He swore he didn't know what happened after that. After he left Billy's, he'd gone to visit a woman friend, who had confirmed that Sam was with her until morning.

Sam claimed his boat had been in dry dock for repairs since late September, and Rick had confirmed that as well. It seemed evident he hadn't killed Bosley unless it had happened before he joined his lady friend, which Rick thought was unlikely. Sam said he'd been home alone on the night Billy was murdered, which meant he didn't have an alibi for the time of his death.

Rick was working the Harvest Festival again today, and Vikki and Brit had volunteered to help out, so George and Meg and Garrett and Clara made the trip out to Skull Island with us. And Kizzy too, of course.

As it had been the day before, the weather was perfect. A slight breeze kept things cool, while there was plenty of sunshine to brighten everyone's day.

"It's been a long time since I've been out on the water," Garrett said. He, Meg, Clara, and I were sitting on the deck, while George rode inside with Jack as he manned the boat. "I forgot how much I enjoy it."

"I'm sure Jack will be happy to take you out anytime you like. We were just talking about the fact that we needed to get out more."

"How much farther is it to Skull Island?" Clara asked.

"About thirty minutes," Meg answered. "We'll need to circle around and put down anchor on the far side, so it'll take a few more minutes to do that."

"There isn't a dock to tie up to?" Clara asked.

"Not anymore."

"Jack has a dinghy to shuttle us to shore," I added.

"Will it accommodate my wheelchair?" Garrett asked. "I'm a little concerned about getting around on the sand."

"It will," I assured him.

"There should still be hardpacked dirt roads on the island," Meg said. "You should be fine."

"I'm anxious to see this lighthouse I've been hearing about," I said. "We never did find out how the last lighthouse keeper died. It seems that might be tied in to whatever else went on at the end."

"I suppose he could have been a witness to what happened," Garrett agreed. "If there was a mass extermination, whoever was responsible wouldn't have wanted to leave behind a witness."

"I'm still having a hard time accepting something like that could have occurred," I said. "It's too barbaric to even consider."

"Maybe it didn't happen that way. We're really just guessing," Garrett reminded me.

"True." I looked at Clara. "Do you think you'll be able to sense what happened?"

"Perhaps. It sometimes works that way. At other times, not so much. I'm not sure, but I hope to get a reading."

"I'm sure it would be pretty awful to experience something like that, even if it's at a distance of a hundred years."

Garrett steered the conversation to our Halloween dinner, a much more cheerful subject. We discussed meal options, debating a few alternates to the nachos appetizer I'd originally suggested, until the island came into view. As we approached the land, which was rocky on the backside, Jack slowed, then turned the boat to circle the island and found a safe place to anchor. When the boat was secure, we set about gathering together everything we'd need on shore. Jack estimated that with Garrett's wheelchair, six people, and the picnic supplies, we'd need to make two trips on the dinghy. George, Clara, and Garrett and his wheelchair went first. Then Jack returned for Meg, me, Kizzy, and the picnic supplies.

"Wow. This place is really something," I said as I stood in the middle of the beach and took in the view. The vegetation had gone unchecked for nearly a century, so it was lush and overgrown. It was going to be harder for Garrett to get around than we'd anticipated. We decided Clara would wait with him in the shady spot we chose for our picnic while the rest of us hiked to the lighthouse.

"Are you sure you want to wait here?" Jack asked a final time before we set off on the hike we estimated would take close to two hours round trip. "I can run you back to the boat. It'll be a lot more comfortable there."

Clara looked at Garrett. "What do you think?"

"I'm fine here. Is the lawn chair we brought for you okay? If you think it won't be comfortable, we can go back."

"I'm fine," Clara said. "I can get up and walk around if need be."

"There's no cell reception out here, so you won't be able to contact us, but we'll hurry," I promised.

Fortunately, George and Meg were in excellent shape despite their age, so they were mostly able to keep up with the pace Jack, Kizzy, and I set. I'd noticed George was having more off days recently, so I kept a close eye on him as we went, but today he seemed lighthearted and energetic. It was probably good for him to get out. He'd spent way too much time indoors lately, trying to solve Bosley's murder.

"I didn't expect to find so many structures still standing," I said as we walked along what would have at one time been a main road running through the small colony. While almost every building still standing had suffered from some amount of decay, I guess I was expecting to find them completely flattened.

"There are those who believe some of the inhabitants of the island stayed and rebuilt after the hurricane," Meg said. "I suppose a lot of what we see now are those buildings, replaced or repaired."

"Why do you think everyone left?" I asked.

"From the accounts I've read, it sounded as if most of the people who lived here died during the hurricane," Meg said. "I'd always thought those who survived didn't have the heart to stay."

I supposed I understood that. If I lost most of my family and friends in a tragedy, it would make sense to want to start over elsewhere. Plus, it must have been in the back of everyone's mind that something like a hurricane could happen again. Better to head to the mainland, where the risk of weather-related tragedies were decreased.

"If some people did stay on Skull Island to rebuild, are we thinking they were still here when Oswald Bollinger arrived with his test subjects?" I asked.

"Good question," George responded. "If there was an existing group of people on the island, I wonder what happened to them. Were they killed as well?"

My stomach was beginning to churn at the thought of what must have gone on during that very dark time. Of course, we had yet to find irrefutable evidence that anything like what we suspected actually happened.

"We should reach the lighthouse in the next fifteen or twenty minutes," Jack said. "I'm not sure we'll find anything there, but it seems as good a place as any to begin our search."

"There must be a cemetery," Meg said. "If we can find it, we might learn something about the culture of the island."

"If what we think happened really did, don't you think everyone would have been buried in a mass grave?" I asked.

"Maybe. But there would have been centuries of people living and dying on the island before that. Of course, if the grave markers no longer remain, it would be hard to know where the cemetery might have been."

We stopped talking as we began to go up to the top of the bluff where the lighthouse had been. It was a steep climb, although there were old stone steps to aid us. When we reached the top, we paused to look at what was left.

"Do you think it's safe to go inside?" Meg asked.

The structure had been made of wood and stone and looked sturdy enough, but it hadn't been maintained in almost a century, so who knew what sort of shape it was in.

While the building was made of stone, the door was wooden. Jack pulled it open and peered inside. "It looks like we'll have to climb to really see anything. All I see now is a stone stairway."

"Seems risky," Meg said.

"Maybe." Jack took a step inside. "I'm going to check it out. You all wait here. That way if I get into trouble, you can save me."

I called Kizzy to me and made her sit and wait at my feet. She wasn't happy to be left behind, and to be honest, I wasn't that happy about waiting behind while Jack risked his life in the old structure either, but it did make sense that most of us wait outside. If there was anything to see, Jack would find it. And while there wasn't any reception on the island, Jack had his phone, so he could take photos of anything he thought might be important.

After a few minutes, he stuck his head out from an opening about three quarters of the way up. "I found the main living area. I'm going to take a look around."

"Take photos," I called up.

Jack pulled his head back inside, and Meg, George, Kizzy, and I continued our wait. Kizzy was restless with Jack gone, so I found a stick and gave it a toss. She took off after it as if her world was once again a better place.

"I hope the place doesn't come down around Jack before he can get out of there," I fretted.

"The lighthouse has stood for centuries," George said. "I'm sure it's structurally sound."

"Are you saying that because you believe it to be true or because you don't want me to worry?" I asked.

"Both. I'm sure Jack is being careful. He knows it would be a disaster if one of us sustained an injury all the way out here."

I knew George was right, but I couldn't help but worry a little.

"So the lighthouse keeper actually lived here, up in that tiny area?" I asked, mostly to keep my mind off Jack and the danger he was putting himself in.

"That's what I understand," Meg replied. "Lighthouse keepers used to rotate quite often, so no one person was stationed there for too long. Still, it must have been cramped and lonely. Of course, during the day, when the weather was good and the light wasn't needed, they would be free to wander around the island."

"That might have provided comfort when a colony of settlers lived here, but once they left?" I shuddered to think how freaky it would be to live alone on the island, and wondered if being alone would be better or worse than living with the people Oswald Bollinger brought here.

"I found a room above the opening for the light," Jack called down. "I'm going to check it out, then come down."

Above the light? I looked up at the cylindrical building. Why would anyone put a room above the light? How would you even get up there? I guessed there might be a ladder.

It seemed it was quite a while later before Jack finally reappeared. I let out a breath of relief when he finally emerged from the building. "Did you find anything?" I asked.

"Actually, I did."

"Something bad?"

Jack nodded. "The little room above the light was, I think, built as a secret of sorts. Perhaps it was somewhere for the keeper to hide if the island was invaded. I can't be certain of its purpose, but you can't see the room from the living area. You have to actually go into the space for the light and look up; only then is the trapdoor visible. It was tricky to get up there, but when I managed to get there, I found a windowless, empty room. I can't imagine it being used for anything except temporary refuge."

"That doesn't sound so bad," I said.

"There's more. Carved into the wall were the words, 'Today is the day we die. God help us all.' It was dated November 12, 1924."

I put my hand to my mouth.

"So there *was* a massacre," George said.

"So it would seem. I'm sure if we had the time to really look around, we'd find that mass grave we talked about. And I'm curious where Bollinger's lab was. It would seem it would have to be a large and much more modern building than the partially decayed structures we saw on our way here."

"I'd be willing to bet the lab, along with anything else that would serve as evidence to what happened here was destroyed," Meg said.

Jack nodded. "Yes, that makes sense. Let's go back and see how Garrett and Clara are doing."

When we got there, they had their own tale to tell, so we spread out a blanket and settled down to eat the sandwiches we'd brought with us.

"I had a vision after you left," Clara said. "It was truly horrifying. I have no doubt many people were killed on this island. Not just the group we believe Bosley was here to research, but many, many others, men, women, and children, who were massacred at the hands of those who invaded the land they hoped to dominate over the centuries."

"It does seem as if there's a lot of negative energy associated with this place," I agreed. "And Brooke told me this island has witnessed more than one bloodbath."

Clara wiped a tear from her cheek. "So much death. It's hard to even process. But I digress. The main thing I want to share is that in addition to the widespread death and destruction, I picked up on something else. There's a cemetery over that little bluff." Clara pointed to it. "I had an image of a grave. A specific grave among many, so I took a hike there to see what I could find. The vegetation has grown to the point that any grave markers that were ever there can no longer be found, but I somehow knew where I needed to dig. I came back and told Garrett what I'd found, and he used his knife to help me fashion a tool to use to dig into the earth."

"And what did you find?" I asked.

Clara handed George a metal box. It was of sturdy construction and had a heavy lock. It was old and rusty but somehow had endured for however long it had been buried. There was no way to know for certain when it had been put in the ground, but it seemed it must be a piece of the puzzle, and I was anxious to find out what was inside.

"Do you know what's in it?" George asked.

"No," Clara admitted. "The vision led me to it, but it didn't provide any clues to what we'd find inside."

George turned the box over in his hands. "To open it, we'll need tools we don't have here. We'll take it with us."

"What did you find?" Garrett asked as soon as we decided to take the box with us.

Jack took the lead to explain. He'd taken a lot of photos of the interior of the lighthouse with his phone, which he passed around. We all wondered whether the lighthouse keeper might have made it off the island alive. I didn't think we'd ever know. One thing was certain: If he did manage to escape what we believed was the murder of all the island's other inhabitants, he hadn't stuck around. Not that I blamed him; I would have been on the next boat off the island as well.

"Look at this." Garrett pointed to one of the photos Jack had taken. We could just make out a series of marks carved into the wall of the main living area of the lighthouse.

"Do they mean something to you?" Jack asked.

"I think it's Morse Code. I'm pretty rusty at it, but I have a book that will translate it at the house." Garrett pointed to a specific section of a wall. "See this here? I think it says something about demons."

"Demons?" I asked.

Jack frowned. "I suppose people who heard voices and talked to themselves might seem like demons to someone who had no background with mental illness."

I felt excitement rise in my chest. "Maybe if we can translate what's written on the walls, we'll have the rest of the story." I looked at George. "Do you think Bosley knew Morse Code?"

"It's possible he might have had a general grasp of it."

I held my hands together. "So if the code on the walls included damaging information, he might recognize it as such."

George nodded. "Yes, I believe he could have."

I turned to look at Jack. "Did you take photos of all the walls?"

"I think so. If it looks as if I missed something, I can always come back. I'd go back now to take a second set of photos just to be sure, but it's getting late. The sun sets earlier this time of year. We should probably go."

While we hadn't found a smoking gun, we had the box Clara had seen in her vision and the writing on the walls. I felt optimistic we'd learn what had gotten Bosley killed at last.

Chapter 9

The day had grown dark by the time we returned to the resort. Clara invited everyone to the main house for dinner. As she tossed together a casserole and a salad, I called to invite Brit and Vikki to join us. Jack set about opening the metal box, while Garrett found his book on Morse Code. There was a feeling of anticipation in the air. We had no idea what we'd find in the box—for all we knew, it could have been the body of a child's pet—but we hoped it would be a significant find.

******

"So someone buried a copy of the contract between Oswald Bollinger and the four members of the island council in the cemetery," I said when the others and Rick had arrived, the box had been opened, and the paper studied. "Why?"

"Someone might have wanted to be sure proof of the agreement wasn't destroyed when things started to go badly and buried it where no one would look," George said.

I supposed that made sense, but who was that *someone*? It surely wouldn't have been Bollinger. In fact, my guess would be that once things began to go south, he most likely packed up and went back to wherever he'd come from in the first place.

"According to this document, the amount of money Bollinger gave to each of the council members was significant," George continued. "In fact, I would go so far as to say the payout was most likely the foundation for the fortunes of all four families."

"I really don't get it," I said with a frown. "Why did they pay them anything? Did they control Skull Island as well as Gull Island?"

"Actually, they did," Meg said. "When the founding fathers landed on Gull Island, they established settlements on Skull, Sanctuary, and Treasure Islands as well. The four islands were only short boat rides from one another. Gull Island was the farthest to the west and closest to the mainland, so it grew the fastest and ended up with the largest population. By the time Bollinger came along, Sanctuary Island, the farthest to the east, was all but deserted. It never really did develop due to its rough terrain. Treasure Island grew parallel to Gull Island and continued to boom, and Skull Island, which once had a large settlement, was all but deserted after the hurricane. My guess is, Bollinger needed an isolated piece of land to establish his laboratory, and Skull Island fit the bill."

"So the island council struck up a deal with this madman who happened to have a lot of cash that made them all rich men," I restated.

"Exactly," George confirmed.

"I imagine if word got out today that the fortunes these four men possess was built on the blood of innocent men and women, there might be some fallout," I added.

"Possibly," George agreed.

"So we're back to Sam Castle, Ron Remand, Zane Carson, and Billy Waller as suspects in Bosley's murder, and Sam Castle, Ron Remand, and Zane Carson as suspects in Billy Waller's," I pointed out. "They seem to have had the most to lose if Bosley made public that their grandfathers or great-grandfathers knew about and profited from atrocities committed against innocent people."

"The problem is, I've cleared all but Billy of Bosley's murder," Rick said. "Sam was with his lady friend, Zane was out of town, and Ron had out-of-town company for the weekend staying at his home, which he never left."

"So maybe Billy killed Bosley, then someone else killed Billy," Vikki said.

"It could have happened that way," Rick admitted. "Although if you ask me, Billy didn't seem like a killer."

"But if not Billy, who?" Brit wondered.

The room fell silent. If Billy's death turned out not to be related to Bosley's, it was conceivable the motive for each was something other than the terrible secret we'd uncovered. I didn't know Bosley well; for all I knew, he could have racked up any number of people who wanted him dead over the years. And

Billy was seen dining with his ex-business partner shortly before his death. That meeting could be a motive as well.

"Did you ever talk to Vincent O'Brian?" I asked Rick

"I did. He said Billy was looking into a new development in Charleston and wanted to know if he had any experience working with the man who was putting together the investment team. Vincent had worked with him a couple of times and was going to be on the island anyway, so he agreed to have dinner with Billy to fill him in on the good and bad aspects of going into business with him. Apparently, the conversation was intense at times because of the topic, but there were never any hard feelings between them, even after their venture failed, and at no time did the meeting that night turn negative."

"And you believe there really were no hard feelings between them?" Brit asked.

Rick nodded. "Vincent seemed sincere—and pretty broken up that Billy is dead."

"So, assuming someone intentionally ran Billy off the road to kill him, they must have known he was at the restaurant," I said. "It would seem it happened right after he left the restaurant."

"I've interviewed staff and no one saw anything that stood out. The restaurant doesn't have a security camera, but I asked them to try to remember who was there at the same time as Billy and Vincent. But it's a big place, and it was a Friday night, so it was busy."

I noticed the frown on Rick's face. "What is it?" I asked.

"The more I think about it, the more it seems the motive for Bosley's death must have been this huge secret he uncovered. I'm going to recheck alibis. Sam said Bosley was alive when he left Billy's, but he didn't have any proof to offer. Billy's dead, so he can't corroborate Sam's statement, and for all I know, the woman he said he was with might be lying for him. Zane said he was out of town and Ron said he had company, but that doesn't really mean one of them couldn't have either snuck away and taken care of the threat to their family reputation or hired someone to do it for them."

"How much do you think it would actually hurt them if the truth came out?" Brit asked. "It's not like they did anything personally. They certainly can't be held responsible for what their great-grandfathers did."

"No, but there could be other fallout," Rick said. "A lot of people on the island have been campaigning for quite some time to do away with the four founders' seats on the council and make all of them elected. Despite the pride many of us feel in the founders and want to see the tradition continue, it seems the campaign to eliminate hereditary membership on the council is growing stronger. A scandal like this, coming right out of the founding families, could be just enough to tip the scales and bring true democracy to the council."

"I think Jessica Carson might have known the secret," I said. "I spoke to her at the kiddie carnival. Initially, she was very open about the founding families and their traditions, but when our conversation segued to Billy's death, and I mentioned that he and Bosley might have been killed because of a secret they both knew, she got this look."

"A look?" Vikki asked.

"An awareness crossed her face, as if something had occurred to her. She changed the subject immediately. I'm certain she must have realized who might have killed Billy, or at least why he might have died."

"I'll have a chat with her," Rick said.

"And Viv Marsh, who's Sam Castle's sister, is the one who first mentioned a scientist who brought people to the island to experiment on them," I added.

"I guess it makes sense that a family secret would be known by all the members of the families," George said.

"Jessica told me all the founding fathers had a lot of children who had a lot of children down through the years. Even though the only ones to have any real power were the eldest sons, there must be dozens of people still living on Gull Island descended from the original four. I wonder how many of them know the secret, how many might have reason to want the secret to stay buried."

"Jill makes a good point," Brit said. "We've been focusing on the founding grandsons who currently hold seats on the council, but what about their siblings or children? Any of them might have motives to protect their family name."

Rick shrugged. "That would open up the suspect pool to half the people on the island."

Rick was right. Widening our suspect list would make it useless.

"What about the Morse Code?" Jack asked. "Do the marks on the lighthouse wall help up at all?"

"I'm still working on it," Garrett said. "A lot of the photos are blurry, but I imagine the lighthouse keeper was keeping a record of his last days. He may even have been using the light to send out messages in the hope of getting help. So far, what I've been able to determine from the code is that demons had been brought to the island, and while initially they were locked up, they mutated and got free."

"Mutated?" I asked.

"*Mutated* wasn't the word the lighthouse keeper used, but he keeps saying the sickness is getting worse, the demons becoming more violent. I don't think the marks on the walls will tell us who killed either Bosley or Billy, but they seem to verify that experiments went on and at some point things began to go wrong."

"Maybe whatever was done to the people made them violent," Brit hypothesized.

"That would be my guess," Garrett said.

I took a deep breath, then let it out slowly. "Where does this leave us? We've uncovered the same horrific secret Bosley did, something so unbearable I'm having a hard time even making sense of it, but we still don't know who killed him or Billy."

"There are a lot of people on Gull Island who'd probably like to keep this a secret," George said. "The secret as motive isn't going to help us a whole lot."

"So who would have the most to lose if it got out?" Jack asked.

Again, no one had anything to say.

Finally, I broke the silence. "Brooke made it sound as if Viv Marsh freely shared her knowledge of what happened all those years ago. It didn't seem she felt threatened by it in any way. She's Sam's sister, and Sam was with Bosley the night he died, the only survivor of the three men who met that night. That should make him a prime suspect, but if Viv isn't concerned about the secret getting out, would Sam be?"

"I suppose if my great-grandfather was part of a mass killing that became the source of my family's fortune, I might not want it getting out, but I don't think I'd kill anyone over it," Brit commented. "Sure, there'd be embarrassment and maybe even some backlash in the short term, but I can't see how it would make a long-term difference in my life."

"Unless it affected your seat on the island council and that seat was important to you," Jack said. He looked at Garrett. "In your opinion, who's the most invested in his seat?"

Garrett thought about it for a moment before he answered. "I guess Zane Carson. Ron is more about his family money than he is about the power that comes with being a Remand. In fact, he's missed more meetings than he's showed up for. Billy used his vote to try to help the island as a whole, but I never got the impression he cared about being on the council that much. Sam used to play the part of founding descendant pretty well, but ever since he divorced his wife, he's seemed more interested in having fun."

"One of the candidates for the elected seats, Glen Pierson, is being endorsed by the Castle Foundation," I said.

"Maybe, but Sam doesn't run the foundation," Garrett informed me. "Bianca, his ex-wife, does. I think the only reason Sam got involved in politics was because she had big plans for him. It may look as if Sam is the prime suspect, but I don't see him caring enough about what it would do to his social standing if the secret got out to commit murder."

"That fits in a way. If the secret was a huge deal to the Castle heirs, why would Viv have brought it up to anyone?"

"So it sounds as if, of the four, Zane Carson is the one who'd care most about what the revelation of the secret might do to his reputation, power, and prestige," Jack said.

"Of the four, I'd say that's true," Garrett replied.

Rick stood up. "I'm going to dig into his alibi a little more. I'll pull phone records and check his financials. If he's the one behind this, I'll prove it."

Chapter 10

Tuesday, October 30

It took a couple of days for Rick to weed through things and recheck motives and alibis, but when he came back to the group, he again told us it wasn't likely Sam Castle, Ron Remand, or Zane Carson killed Bosley. Billy could still have been responsible for Bosley's death, Rick admitted, but his gut told him that he wasn't. And, with the added complication that someone had killed Billy shortly after, we all felt, when we met around the fire on Monday night, we were no closer to figuring out who'd killed Bosley than we were at the very beginning.

"We need some additional photos of the decorations the merchants have put up for our *Halloween on Gull Island* spread tomorrow," I said to Jack as we worked to format the newspaper's weekly edition.

"It would be nice to have a photo of Meg's village, and Bernie over at the dry cleaner went all-out with lights this year." Jack paused and looked down at Kizzy, who was staring intently at him. "I guess we can take a break and maybe take Kizzy for a walk through town to get some additional images. We can grab some lunch while we're out."

"I am hungry. And I still need to get some small pumpkins and other accents for the centerpiece for the table for Wednesday's dinner. Maybe we can park near the Halloween store so we can pick up what we need. That deli with the homemade soups is just down the block from there, and they have a dog-friendly patio."

"It does seem to be unseasonably warm today."

"Indian summer," I said. "I think the mild temps are supposed to last all week."

"Just let me save what I have here and we can go," Jack said.

I went into the bathroom to wash up while he finished what he was doing. I was curious whether Rick had dug up anything new on either death since we'd met the previous evening. It seemed unlikely— it had only been half a day—but he'd said he had an idea he was going to follow up on before he was ready to talk about it. Being the inquisitive person I am, his comment had planted itself in my imagination immediately, and I'd been wondering about it ever since.

"Are you ready?" Jack asked when I returned to the reception area, where we'd been working.

"Yes. Do you have Kizzy's leash?"

Jack held it up.

"Remind me to look for cornstalks for the front porch while we're shopping. I think they had some at the feedstore. Of course, it's two days before Halloween, so they may have sold out."

We went to the park first to let Kizzy take care of her needs, then headed to the seasonal store, which still had some Halloween items, and parked near the front door. Kizzy was a well-behaved dog who was welcome at most of the shops in town, so we hooked up her leash and went inside. Jack and Kizzy took a basket and went in search of small pumpkins to use as accents while I strolled up and down the mostly bare aisles, looking for inspiration.

I hadn't actually planned to combine holiday shopping with sleuthing until I saw Jessica Carson, contemplating a bin filled with rubber spiders.

"The one with the flashing red eyes is pretty terrifying," I said as I stopped next to her.

She turned and looked in my direction. "I had my eye on it, but the one with the crooked grin looks a little more approachable for my nephew's party."

"I'm assume you're decorating for a Halloween party?" I asked conversationally.

"Actually, it's my nephew's birthday party. He'll be ten and he wanted to do a spooky house because his birthday happens to be on Halloween."

"Oh," I said. "I know you said you were Zane's sister, but I wasn't aware he had young children."

Jessica tossed both spiders in her basket. "He doesn't. His children are all adults with children of their own. This nephew is my sister Patricia's son. If you remember, I told you Zane and I share a father but not a mother; Patricia and I share a mother but not a father." She laughed. "I'm afraid my family tree is about as confusing as it gets, but it works for us." Jessica glanced at my basket. "It looks like you're doing some decorating as well."

"I'm giving a dinner party on Halloween for the writers who live at the retreat. I decided a special centerpiece is a must, but things are pretty picked over by now. I should have shopped earlier, but between the Harvest Festival and our investigation…" I intentionally let that dangle. I couldn't help but notice Jessica averted her eyes. I was sure she knew something, I just needed to find a way to get her to tell me about it. "Is Zane back in town?" I asked.

Jessica shrugged. "Who knows with him? He's popped in and out on a frequent but random basis since his divorce. If you want to talk to him, you should text or call, although I think he might be out of town at the moment. The last time I spoke to him was on the Saturday before last. He'd just returned from one trip and was already talking about another." Jessica sighed. "Sometimes I envy him his freedom, but other times I worry about him. I think he's been lonely since his wife took off."

Jessica glanced at me, then blushed. "Sorry. I don't suppose I should be talking to you about Zane's personal life. You don't even know him, do you? I've just been worried about him lately, and you're a good listener." Jessica looked at the clock that hung on a nearby wall. "I should get going. Enjoy your dinner party."

I watched her walk to the front of the store where the checkout counters were located.

If Zane had just come home from a trip a week ago Saturday, that meant he very likely was in town when Bosley was killed. I took out my phone and texted Rick, letting him know what I'd just discovered. He texted back that he was out on a call but would get back to me when he was in his office. We'd agreed that of the four men on the island council, Zane was the most likely to care about a family secret getting out. Maybe he'd come home from his trip to take care of the potential leak, then left again before anyone even knew he'd been here.

"Find what you need?" Jack asked when he and Kizzy joined me near the spiders.

"I got sidetracked." I took a moment to explain.

"It's interesting that Zane might have been here the day Bosley's body was most likely dumped in the ocean, but we still wouldn't know who killed Billy."

I bit my lower lip. "I'm not sure yet, but I sure would like to figure that out."

******

After we made our way around town taking photos and gathering the supplies I needed, we went to the deli for lunch. I ordered a thick meatball soup with half a turkey sandwich, while Jack chose a meatball sub with chicken noodle soup. Kizzy crawled under the table as she'd been trained to do, waiting for us to eat and hoping one or both of us saved her a bite.

Rick texted me again just after we sat down. I told him where we were, and he asked us to sit tight and he'd join us in a minute. He indicated he had news to share, which I hoped meant he'd cracked things wide open.

"Sorry, just the opposite," Rick said after he took a seat and ordered his own lunch. "I spoke to Zane, who said he'd been in Florida until Friday, then drove home. He arrived late, after midnight, and went straight to bed. He spoke to Jessica on Saturday morning, when she'd called to check on him as she often did, and he told her he was flying out the next day for a reunion with some old friends. Zane was able to produce gas receipts from his drive from Key West to Gull Island, as well as an airline ticket to Minnesota, where he met his friends for a fishing expedition. Unless he killed Bosley in the middle of the night when he got home, which I suppose is possible but not likely, I don't think he's our guy."

"Drat. I really thought it might be him. Any new leads?"

"Maybe."

I sat up straighter. "Tell!"

"I spoke to Kaitlin Longtree, who lives next door to Meg's friend Lily, who told us that she saw Bosley and Sam at Billy's house on the evening Bosley died. She confirmed she saw Bosley's vehicle in Billy's drive as well. She'd never met Bosley, so she didn't know it was his, but when I described the car, she confirmed that was the vehicle in Billy's drive from around sunset until after she went to bed. She also said it was gone the following morning."

"Okay, we definitely know Bosley was at Billy's. Did she see Sam's car as well?"

"She did. And, like Lily, she confirmed that while Sam was at the house for a while, she didn't think it was more than an hour or two. Nothing bad had happened yet, so she didn't have reason to pay a lot of attention to the timeline, just as Lily didn't, but she had something to add that Lily either hadn't noticed or didn't think was worth mentioning."

"And what was that?" I asked.

"Shortly after Sam left, another vehicle drove up. She didn't see who was behind the wheel—it was completely dark by then—but she noticed it was a dark-colored sports car. Maybe a Corvette, although she admitted to not being much of an expert on cars. She thought it was black, dark blue, or dark gray."

"Do we know whose car it was?"

"Not yet, but I'm working on it."

"Was the car there long?" Jack asked.

"Ms. Longtree saw the car pull in to the drive, then drive around to the back. She had no idea when the car left."

I sat back in my chair and crossed my arms over my chest. "So maybe it was the person in the sports car who killed Bosley."

"And maybe Billy was a witness. He might have promised not to tell, then developed a conscience, and he was killed to silence him," Jack added.

"That's my favorite theory," Rick said. "Now we just need to figure out who drives a dark-colored sports car that may or may not be a Corvette."

We finished lunch and Rick went back to work, while Jack, Kizzy, and I returned to the newspaper. Rick would be pulling DMV records pertaining to individuals who owned dark-colored Corvettes, and Jack and I had a newspaper to get ready for printing. If the Corvette search didn't turn up any leads, he planned to do a search for other vehicles of similar size and body style.

I took Kizzy into the back room to give her a fresh bowl of water while Jack checked the messages on the answering machine and in the paper's e-mail account. When I joined him he was staring at the phone with a frown on his face.

"Is there a problem?" I asked.

"There was a message from Bianca Castle. She wants to take out a full-page ad in tomorrow's paper for her candidate, Glen Pierson."

I narrowed my gaze. "A full-page ad? That seems like overkill. Besides, we already have the paper formatted. Where would we add a full-page ad?"

"She wanted page one or two. There's no way I'm going to run an ad on the front page, and page two and three have already been set aside for the Halloween piece. I suppose we could give her page four and move everything back a page, but I'm not sure how I feel about running a political ad."

"Are you afraid it will look as if we're endorsing Pierson?"

Jack nodded. "Kind of. Especially because all we've had in the paper so far have been impartial articles about the campaign. So far, all the candidates have had equal time."

"So tell her no. It isn't as if you need the money the ad would bring in."

Jack leaned a hip against the desk. "I'll call her. Maybe I can help her to see our position without making her mad. It wouldn't benefit us to make an enemy who wields as much power as she does."

"Why does she wield so much power?" I asked. "She isn't married to Sam anymore. Why is she even running the family foundation?"

Jack shrugged. "I'm not sure. Maybe Garrett or someone who's been around longer than we have would know."

I was curious enough to wonder at the dynamics involved. Somehow, ex-wives and family politics seemed like a Brooke thing, so I texted her to ask if I could come by to chat with her after school let out.

******

"Sam Castle wasn't in to politics until Bianca came into his life," Brooke explained almost an hour after I texted her. "In fact, there was talk that he wasn't going to accept the seat on the council despite tradition when his father decided to retire."

"So Bianca isn't a local girl?"

Brooke shook her head. "Sam met Bianca, who was a beautiful, vivacious woman by any standards, while vacationing in the Bahamas. I guess it was love at first sight, because they were married just months after they met. They seemed to be a fairy-tale couple: young and rich and good-looking. Even Sam's dad, who hadn't liked Bianca at first and had thought she was a gold digger, changed his tune when he saw she was not only beautiful but strong-willed, and had political aspirations for Sam."

"It sounds as if both Bianca and her new father-in-law had plans for Sam that might not have been his own."

Brooke nodded. "Exactly. Bianca is very persuasive, and Sam was putty in her hands. He began to show an interest in the island council, and when his father retired, he happily took his place. It was Bianca who created the Castle Foundation; a charitable foundation for sure, but one that was also self-serving, if you ask me. On the surface, it appeared Sam was in the driver's seat, but it was Bianca running the show all along."

"Then what happened?" I asked.

"Sam met Angelica."

"The woman he's involved with now?"

Brooke nodded. "He seems to be in love with her, although I think she's as much of a user as Bianca. I doubt it will work out in the long run, but Angelica managed to open Sam's eyes to what he was missing. Bianca moved out, and Sam filed for divorce. Part of her settlement was that she'd retain her position as executive director of the Castle Foundation. I'm sure you realize she's compensated very well for her role with the organization. She uses the Castle name to gain contributors and to give the organization legitimacy."

"So Glen Pierson is Bianca's candidate. She plans to use and control him the way she used and controlled Sam," I said.

Brooke nodded. "Bianca still needs Sam—or at least she needs the reputation the Castle name provides for her—so she hasn't done anything to completely sever ties with him. Sam divorced her, but it was all quite amicable. Bianca is doing what many first wives do: rule in a man's world by having a man as a figurehead."

"I guess I can see why she's so pushy. Thanks, Brooke. You've filled in a few gaps for me."

I was just returning to the truck when Jack texted to ask if I could stop by Bianca's to pick up the feature that would be published instead of the ad she'd wanted to run. I asked him why she couldn't just e-mail it, and he texted again to say she wanted to take a couple of photos to be used in place of the campaign photos she'd planned to run. Jack had somehow managed to talk Bianca into trading a full-page ad for her candidate for a full-page article describing the work being done by the Castle Foundation. Way to find a compromise!

Chapter 11

Bianca Castle lived in an oceanfront estate just north of Gull Island. The grounds were gorgeous. Not quite as large and opulent as the one Sam still lived on, but very, very nice indeed. Brooke had indicated Bianca pulled in a nice salary from the Castle Foundation, but based on the size and location of her property, I was willing to bet she'd received a nice financial settlement as well.

"You aren't Jackson Jones," Bianca said when she opened the front door in response to my knock.

"I'm Jill Hanford. I work with Jack. He asked me to come by to get the photos because I was already out."

"Very well." Bianca sighed. "Come on in."

I took a step into the large entry hall after Bianca. I was sure Jack must have used his charm to wiggle out of the political ad without angering such a powerful woman, but he may have done too good a job; from the way she was dressed, it appeared she had assumed he was going to take the photos himself and had a few other activities in mind.

"Your home is lovely," I said in an attempt to break the tension that had been created when Bianca realized she wasn't going to have her cake and eat it too.

"Thank you. Are you an experienced photographer?"

I nodded, even though technically I wasn't. "I can promise I'll do a good job. Did you have something specific in mind?"

"I thought we could take the photos in the office where I conduct business. I'd like something professional. A spread that will let the world know we're a serious foundation with serious goals and the means to make them happen."

I held up my camera. "Of course. Lead the way and we'll take a look at what we have to work with."

I followed Bianca down the hallway. Her heels clicked in rhythm on the marble floors as she quickened her pace, which clearly indicated she was a serious woman on a tight schedule and I'd best keep up if I didn't want to be left behind. Upon arriving at the office, which was larger than many people's houses, the first thing I noticed was the floor-to-ceiling fireplace. The second was the wall of photos, which featured, among other images, a large photo of Bianca sitting on the hood of a black Maserati convertible. I supposed to an untrained eye in the dark, a Maserati could be mistaken for a Corvette.

I walked over to the photos. "Nice car."

"Thank you. She was my gift to myself when my divorce became final."

"I love cars, especially sexy sports cars. I don't suppose you'd let me take a peek?"

"I'm afraid she's in the shop. Maybe another time. Now, about the photos you're taking... Perhaps we should start with me sitting behind my desk."

I nodded. "That sounds like a good place to start."

I spent the next twenty minutes snapping photos, making sure I angled the camera to capture the photos on the wall several times. My heart was pounding the entire time as my mind screamed not to give away the fact that I was pretty sure I'd just solved both murders.

"I think that should do it," I said, once again trying to mask my urgency to get out of there.

"Are you sure? We haven't even taken any outdoor shots."

"I think what I have is fine. And I think you'll be pleased with the article. I'll put together the spread as soon as I get back to the newspaper, and either Jack or I will send it over for your approval."

Bianca frowned. "Is there something wrong? You seem a little fidgety."

I shook my head. "No. Nothing's wrong. I just have a lot to do today. You know how it is on the day before going to print. There are always last-minute details to take care of."

Bianca raised a perfectly shaped brow. "I see. Well, if you're sure you have everything...I'll walk you out."

"No need," I said much too quickly. "I can find my way."

I was halfway down the hall when I heard Bianca call my name. I cringed, then turned around, half-expecting her to have a gun at my back. Wasn't that the way these things usually went in the movies? The heroine figures out who the killer is, then ends up with her life on the line. Instead, Bianca was holding the lens cap of my camera.

"Oh, geez, thank you," I said as I headed back down the hallway toward the woman I was certain had killed two people. "I wouldn't want to forget that."

Bianca frowned. From the expression on her face, my behavior was setting off some alarms in her head. "No, I guess not."

I took a slow breath. "And thank you again. It's been lovely meeting you."

I turned and walked slowly down the hall, almost waiting to hear the sound of a shot as it stole my life, ending once and for all what might have been.

******

"Okay, slow down," Rick said twenty minutes later as I tried to explain what I'd discovered. "Are you saying Bianca Castle pulled a gun on you?"

I shook my head. "No. But she seemed suspicious, and I felt as if she might pull a gun on me."

Rick furrowed his brow. "So, she didn't have a weapon, but you're terrified anyway because you imagined she might."

"Exactly."

Rick leaned back and crossed his arms over his chest. "Maybe you should back up a bit, because so far, this isn't making any sense."

I took a long drink from the glass of water Rick had poured for me when I'd first arrived. I'd had the entire drive over to imagine what could have happened and was pretty rattled.

"I talked to Brooke, who told me it was Bianca who actually started the Castle Foundation. She was also the force behind Sam's political career while they were married, and the one who seemed to have the most ambition."

Rick nodded. "I agree with that assessment. But what does that have to do with you thinking she was going to pull a gun on you?"

"You said at lunch that Billy's neighbor saw a car that might be a Corvette pull into Billy's drive after Sam left. When I was at Bianca's, I noticed a photo of a black Maserati on the wall of her office. I could see how it could look like a Corvette to an inexperienced eye in the dark."

"You think it was Bianca who was at Billy's the night Bosley died?"

I nodded my head. "It makes sense. We know Sam and Bianca continued to have a relationship of some sort after their divorce. And that Bosley had spoken to Sam about his research before the night he died. What if Sam told Bianca what Bosley was up to? What if on the night Billy called Sam to come over, he was with Bianca? What if she knew where he was going and why, and followed him? If the scandal regarding the founding families came out, it stands to reason the fallout could affect the Foundation, which was Bianca's baby. What if after Sam left, Bianca confronted Bosley? What if she killed him, and convinced poor Billy to help her dispose of the body? What if Billy's conscience got the better of him, and he told Bianca he was going to tell what he knew?

What if Bianca followed him to the restaurant and killed him when he left?"

"That's a lot of *what ifs*, but your theory might hold water. Do you have any proof?"

"No. But Bianca told me that her car was in the shop. Find the car and find your proof."

Rick frowned. "Bianca might have driven the car to Billy's on the night Bosley died, but it's doubtful she drove it again the night Billy died. Remember how hard it was raining?"

"Okay, check all her cars. I have to believe somewhere you'll find the proof you need to put her away."

Rick paused, steepling his fingers and rocking gently in his chair. "Okay. I like your theory. I'll work on getting a warrant for Bianca's home, her garage, and her vehicles."

Chapter 12

Wednesday, October 31

"I'd like to make a toast," Vikki said after standing and clicking a knife on her glass. "To my best friend Jill, who managed to make sense of a lot of random clues and solved the mystery of the murders of Bosley and Billy Waller. And to my boyfriend and new roomie, Rick, who got the warrants he needed to find the proof required to make the arrest, and finally, to George and the rest of you, for uncovering the truth behind a very complicated and long-held secret. You all rock."

"Thanks, Vikki," I said in response. "But you don't need to toast us. You helped too. We all worked together to solve this mystery."

Vikki shrugged. "I know. We all work hard to solve these mysteries, but I noticed we never take a minute to congratulate ourselves on a job well done. I think we should."

"Hear, hear." All of us gathered for our Halloween dinner clicked our glasses together.

"Did Bianca confess?" Garrett asked.

"Not yet," Rick answered. "But I understand her attorney is working on a plea deal. We'll have to see how things works out. There's no doubt in my mind that woman will be going away for a long time."

"I heard Glen Pierson is dropping out of the island council race," Jack said. "Not that I blame him for wanting to distance himself from Bianca and the Castle family."

"So I guess that means Bill Quarterly and Jeffrey Riverton will take the two open seats," Garrett said.

I held up a hand. "What about Brenda Tamari? She's still in the running."

Garrett looked doubtful.

"Well, I'm campaigning for her," I said, although I had no idea how I'd find the time to do it or if it would do any good with the vote so close.

"I'll help you," Gertie volunteered.

"Me too," Vikki said.

"I'll do an e-mail blast," Brit offered.

Jack put his arm around my shoulders. "I'm in. Brenda would be a much better choice than Riverton."

The consensus around the table was that it might be good to see an end to the old boys' club the council had always been.

"What's next for the group?" asked Gertie, who had volunteered to cook the dinner that evening. I had to admit her roast trumped my idea of nachos by a lot. "After the election, that is."

"Maybe we'll take the holidays off and relax a bit," I said.

The others thought that would be nice, though I was aware things usually didn't work out that way. Some time to focus on my relationship with Jack would be welcome, and I knew Vikki and Rick had their own issues to work through and resolve as well.

"Too bad Alex is missing this," Brit said. "This meal is delicious."

"Why, thank you, pumpkin," Gertie said. "The autumn soup is an old family recipe of mine, and the seasoned potatoes I'm servin' with the pot roast is a recipe handed down to Garrett from his great-grandmother."

"Thank you for making them," Garrett said.

"No problem at all. They're goin' to be delicious with Mortie's horseradish gravy."

"*Mortie's* horseradish gravy?" I asked. Mortie was the ghost Gertie claimed had lived in her house for over thirty years.

"Mortie seemed to have been a good cook in life. Several of the specialties I serve at the restaurant are from recipes he's shared with me."

Interesting. Gertie's specials were to die for, no matter where she got them.

"I love the fact that Mortie's legacy lives on through your cooking," Vikki said. "Not everyone can continue to contribute after they're gone."

"I was thinking last night about the people who died on Skull Island," George said. "It's doubtful anyone knew they were there or what happened to them."

"We have the names," I said. "At least some of them, in the register in the church. Maybe we should publish a memorial in the newspaper."

Jack set his napkin aside. "I thought of doing something like that, but what's done can't be undone, and I think stirring things up even more at this point could do harm to innocent people who live and work on the island today. Even the church was probably involved on some level."

"Why do you say that?" Clara asked.

"The register with all those deaths on November 24, 1924, had to have been filled in by someone. Someone who knew what was going on. And the book was found with other church records that indicated that SIRP stood for Skull Island Research Project."

Jack had a point. I hadn't considered that.

"We could go back," Meg suggested. "All of us. We could hold a private service for those who died all those years ago."

"I like that idea," I said.

"Me too," Vikki agreed.

We all agreed to find a day to do that the following week, before the weather got dicey.

After the wonderful meal Gertie had prepared was consumed, we retired to the living room to watch Halloween movies. It was nice being part of a family who were creating new traditions I hoped would see us many years into the future. When I'd come to Gull Island, I wasn't sure what I would find, but in my wildest imagination, I'd never expected to find the piece of my heart that had always been missing.

"So, how do you think our cohabitation experiment is going?" Jack asked as we walked from the main house to his cabin.

"I think it's going very well. I like waking up to Kizzy," I teased.

"And Kizzy likes waking up to you, although I don't think she's thrilled that you've taken over her spot next to me on something of a regular basis."

I shrugged. "I'm sure she'll adjust. She's a good foot warmer, so I'm fine with her at the foot of the bed."

Jack laced his fingers through mine and pulled me closer. "How are you feeling about extending our two-week agreement?"

I paused before answering. "I'm feeling fine about the concept. What did you have in mind?"

"I was thinking it might be less confusing for Kizzy if you moved in permanently."

I glanced down at the dog, who had heard her name and was watching us intently. "I guess it would be a good idea—to make things less confusing for the dog."

Next from Kathi Daley Books

Preview:

Monday, October 22

The thing that hit me hardest as I stood in a dark and dank basement struggling to make sense of a death by vampire less than two weeks before Halloween, was that someone had gone to a lot of trouble to put this whole thing together. A stormy night, a creepy old house, a dog in peril, a body in the basement, and a legendary killer who couldn't possibly be real.

"Walk me through everything that happened from the beginning," Sheriff Salinger, a nemesis turned friend, said to me after he'd covered the body with a white sheet while we waited for the coroner.

I reached up to wipe a spiderweb from my hair before I began to speak. "I was at the Zoo." I referred to Zoe's Zoo, the wild and domestic animal rescue and rehabilitation shelter I owned. "I was about to close up when I got a call about a barking dog that was reportedly trapped inside an abandoned house. Jeremy usually closes up at five, but he was off today. He'd volunteered to chaperone his daughter Morgan's preschool field trip to the pumpkin patch. I remembered doing that when I was a kid. So fun."

"I don't think I need quite that much detail," Salinger said.

"You're right. I'm sorry. The point is, not only was Jeremy off today but it also happens to be

Monday. Aspen's started working Saturdays so we can offer adoption services six days a week. Because she works Saturdays, Aspen has begun to take Mondays off." I could see Salinger was becoming impatient with the details of the lives of my employees, Jeremy Fisher and Aspen Wood, but this part was important. "So not only were Jeremy and Aspen not available to take the call, but my third in command, Tiffany Middleton, who recently married Scott Walden, the veterinarian, and has decided she only wants to work half days. She gets off at two." I paused, giving Salinger time to catch up. "I'm sure you can see where I'm going with this."

"I have no idea where you're going with this," Salinger countered.

I paused as a clap of thunder shook the old wooden structure. If I hadn't been so terrified, I would admire the artistry of the whole thing. I wondered if the storm was just a coincidence, or if whoever put this thing together intentionally waited for one to roll in. I cringed as a second clap of thunder followed the first, then returned my attention to the sheriff. "On almost any other day, there would have been someone else at the Zoo to respond to a routine barking dog call. Someone other than me. The fact that this place," I swept my hand around the room, "is arranged exactly the way it is tells me that whoever killed this man wanted me, and only me, to find the body."

Salinger still looked confused, although I thought I was being quite clear. "Don't you see?" I continued. "A creepy old house, a dog in peril, and a body in the basement. Doesn't it seem just a tiny bit familiar?"

Salinger rubbed his chin with his right hand, as if trying to work through the details with which he'd been presented. After a moment he spoke. "The scene does seem familiar."

"The setup is the same as the scene I found when I stumbled upon the body of Coach Griswold five years ago. The way this body is posed is even the same, although the method of death is most decidedly different."

Salinger bent down for a closer look. He gently lifted the sheet, took a closer look at the victim, and then looked back at me. "So we have a copycat."

"Perhaps. But if I recall correctly, you and I are the only two people to have witnessed the scene of the first crime. I know I didn't set this whole thing up so…" I raised a brow at Salinger.

"Of course I didn't set this up," Salinger huffed. "The details of Coach Griswold's death are in the file. Photos and such. I suppose they could have been leaked at some point. It happens. But my real question is, if someone wanted to get your attention, why did they duplicate this murder? You've been involved in dozens of murder investigations over the years, so why this particular murder out of all the possibilities?"

"I don't know. And I hate idea that a man is dead and it could very well be my fault indirectly, but I really do feel it's possible all this has been arranged for my benefit."

"You think this man was murdered as a prop for whatever sick game someone is playing with you?"

I shrugged. "Maybe. I hope not, but everything about the scene of this murder seems too perfect not to have been intentional. The call about the dog was made anonymously. The person I spoke to said they didn't want to leave a name, but they felt they should call because they were afraid the dog was trapped inside the house. I was the one to respond because I was the only one at the Zoo. When I got here there was a dog in the house, tied up in the basement. I guess whoever set this up wanted to be sure I'd check the basement."

Salinger stood up and took out a notepad. "Where is this dog now?"

"In my car, with Charlie. I didn't want the dogs to have to wait down here with the body." I glanced at the sheet on the floor. "Who do you think it is?"

Salinger shook his head. "I don't know. The victim doesn't have identification on him. I'll run his prints after we get him to the morgue." Salinger used his flashlight to look around the room. The storm had totally blotted out any light that would have been provided by the late afternoon sun, and the only window was a small area of glass high on the wall, at ground level from the outside. "So, if this little murder scene was set up for your benefit do you have any idea *who* might have done it? Any idea at all?"

"Well, my first thought, given the fact that the man seems to have died from a bite to the neck, is Dracula, although I suppose it could have been another vampire altogether."

"Dracula didn't kill this man. A vampire didn't kill this man."

"How do you know?" I asked with a slight lilt to my voice.

Salinger glanced at me. "Dracula isn't real. Vampires aren't real."

I raised a brow. "Then how do you explain the two little puncture wounds in the man's neck? I've watched my share of vampire movies. I know what I'm looking at. Maybe someone I helped send to jail was turned and has come back to enact his revenge."

Salinger chuckled. "*Enact his revenge*. That's precious. While I love your childlike belief in possibilities, I can assure you, a living person killed this man, not an undead creature of the night."

I crossed my arms over my chest. "Okay, then, if not a vampire, who?"

"I don't know. Yet," Salinger said.

I could hear more thunder rolling in from the distance. Charlie wasn't normally the sort to cower when we had lightning storms, but he'd been left in the car with a strange dog after witnessing me have a bit of a freak out when I found the body. I should wrap this up and go check on him.

"You said it seemed the stage had been set for your benefit," Salinger said. "Say that's true. Does anyone come to mind who might be motivated to do all this? Anyone human?"

I let out a little half laugh. "I'll admit that as I was driving out here with the rain pouring down all around my car, I thought it might have been Zak who'd sent me on this fateful mission," I said, referring to my husband, Zak Zimmerman.

Salinger dropped his jaw. "Why on earth would Zak kill a man and then stage this scene for you?"

"Oh, he wouldn't," I quickly answered. "It was just that after I got the barking dog call and realized the dog that was overheard seemed to be trapped in the Henderson House, I remembered I'd received the same call five years ago. As I made my way out here in the middle of a rainstorm, it occurred to me that my very caring and inventive husband might have set up a surprise to try to lure me out of my funk. Not that he would lure me with a dead body, mind you. I didn't know we were dealing with an actual murder until after I got here. But as I made the trip out, it did occur to me that maybe Zak had arranged for me to respond to the same call I did all those years ago to bring some Halloween fun into my life."

"You suspected Zak would send you to a house where you previously found a dead body as a prank?"

"Not a prank exactly. More like a gift. I suspected that when I arrived I'd find a bunch of decorations. Maybe a mannequin mimicking a murder victim."

"I have to say, the two of you are the oddest couple."

"Not odd really," I countered. "Zak knows I usually love Halloween and appreciate a genuine scare. Normally, it wouldn't occur to me that he would go to such lengths, but I'm afraid I've been complaining to anyone who will listen that I'm having a hard time finding the magic of the holiday this year. It seemed like a Zak thing to do to scare the Halloween back into me. He's sweet that way."

Salinger chuckled again before taking out his camera. "I wouldn't be too worried about not feeling the usual magic this year," he said as he began snapping photos. "You do have a lot on your plate, and I suppose at your age, the level of excitement you feel over holidays—or anything, actually—fades somewhat."

I leaned a hip against the wall. "But that's just it. I don't want the fantasy to fade. Yes, I know I have a baby who requires a lot of my attention, and I'm raising two teenagers as well as seeing to Zak's adopted grandmother. I do understand that a certain level of fatigue comes with all that. But I don't want to settle into old ladyhood quite yet. I want to feel happy anticipation. I want to go crazy at the Halloween store picking out decorations, and I want to look forward to the Zoe Donovan Halloween Spooktacular rather than dreading all the extra work it's going to generate. I hate that I find myself wondering if we shouldn't have just skipped the party this year."

Salinger stopped snapping photos. He reached out and put a hand on my arm. "I understand how you feel. I feel the same way sometimes. But you have a long way to go before anyone is going to consider you old. Fatigue might be dimming your enthusiasm right now, but Catherine is getting older, and soon she won't require as much care, and Nona seems to be settling into her new situation."

I let out a sigh. "Yeah, I guess. Zak says I should try to focus on the things in my life that fit the way things are now, like finding a cute costume for Catherine rather than worrying about the fact that I don't have time to organize the zombie run this year. I know he's right. I've never been good with change, and there have been a lot of changes in my life lately."

"I can agree that your life has undergone a lot of change in a short period of time," Salinger said. "But no matter what life throws at you, you're the most capable person I know. Give yourself a break and try to enjoy what you have instead of fretting over what you've had to give up."

I smiled. 'Thanks. That helps. Zak, Levi, and Ellie have all been saying the exact same thing, but somehow it's a bit more convincing coming from you."

Salinger took out a plastic bag and, using a gloved hand, bagged a discarded bottle cap as well as a partially smoked cigarette. "Glad I can help."

I glanced at the door leading out to the hallway. "I can hear a car in the drive."

"It must be the medical examiner. I'll need to chat with him for a while. Why don't you go on home to that family of yours? I think it would be best if you stayed close to home until we get this figured out."

I nodded. "Will you call me when you know whose body it is we found?"

"I will. I'm hoping we know this by evening, but if not, maybe tomorrow morning. Of course, if the man's prints aren't in the system, our job is going to be a whole lot harder. He doesn't look at all familiar to me, so I don't think he's a local. He could just be someone passing through. If I don't get a hit from the fingerprints and he doesn't match any missing persons reports, I'll start looking at the lodging properties in the area."

"If I can help let me know."

"You can't. You're retired from the sleuthing game. Remember?"

I nodded. "I remember. That's just another change I'm trying to get my head around. If I don't hear from you this evening I'll talk to you tomorrow."

After I left the basement I left the house through the rear; the back of the house was the closest to the basement, and suddenly, I felt claustrophobic. It was still raining, but getting wet seemed preferable to spending even one more minute in the stale air that had been trapped inside. I stepped from the small porch into the yard behind the house, turned, and looked back. I knew from previous visits that the structure was two stories, with an attic and a basement. It sat toward the back of a large, overgrown lot surrounded by an iron fence and an impenetrable gate that opened onto a dirt drive leading to a walkway comprised of four rotted steps and an equally rotted porch. The house, once owned by Hezekiah Henderson, certainly had seen more than its share of death.

Hezekiah was already an old man when I was a child. A *crazy* old man, I'd like to add. Although he'd seemed to have adequate financial resources, he'd chosen to live as a recluse who rarely, if ever, left his creepy old house. When I was seven, one of my classmates told me that in his youth, Hezekiah had murdered and then dismembered over a hundred people. It was rumored he'd buried the body parts under the floorboards in the basement and then settled into a life of seclusion to maintain the spell he'd used to trap the souls of his victims in limbo for all time. Of course, I didn't necessarily believe the story to be true, but, like I said, the house had seen more than its share of death. Hezekiah died when I was nine, and for years after that, no one dared enter the creepy place, though as time went by the rumors ceased, and vagrants began to use the building to ward off cold winter nights. The legend of Hezekiah Henderson and the haunted basement faded.

Then, seventeen years ago, a bunch of counselors from a nearby summer camp decided to have a party in the old house. Before the night was over, four counselors were dead. Which brings us to five years ago, when I found Coach Griswold's body in the basement. That murder had had a very human explanation, but that didn't stop a ghost hunter from coming to town four years ago to research paranormal activity in the house. He seemed to be on to some sort of a revelation until his body was found at the bottom of the stairs a few days later.

When I returned to my car my best little pal and constant sidekick, Charlie, was waiting impatiently with the very pregnant cocker spaniel I'd rescued from the house. "I'm sorry it took so long." I grabbed a towel from the back seat and dried my face and hair. "I knew you'd be worried, but having you both wait in the car seemed the best course of action." I looked at the spaniel. "So, what are we going to do with you?" The dog cowered on the back seat, which I guess I understood. The poor thing had probably been dognapped, then tied up in the basement of Henderson House for who knew how long. "I guess I'll take you home until we can find your humans. It looks like those pups could come at any time, and it will be much more comforting to be around people than to be locked up in a pen at the Zoo."

Fortunately, the Zimmerman clan was between fosters. In addition to Charlie, we had two full-time dogs and three full-time cats. More often than not, we also had a dog, a cat, or both, we were fostering as well. Currently, however, the spare room was free of any temporary furry guests. I called the house and spoke to Alex, the fourteen-year-old girl who lived with Zak and me. I told her what had happened and that I was on my way, and she agreed to and start dinner. Scooter, the fourteen-year-old boy who lived with us too, had soccer practice after school, which had been moved to the gymnasium due to the rain. That was where Zak would be picking him up. I was fairly certain both would be home shortly. I'd left my almost-ten-month-old daughter with my best friend, Ellie Denton, so I'd need to stop at the boathouse where Ellie lived with her husband Levi and toddler Eli, before heading home for the evening.

Charlie settled in the front seat and the mama spaniel curled up with the blanket I'd found in my trunk in the back, and I started the car and started slowly down the rutted dirt drive. The pouring rain had created large puddles that I navigated carefully so as not to jostle my pregnant passenger any more than I had to. While the rain was still coming down, it seemed the thunder and lightning had moved on, at least for now. The sky was still heavy with dark clouds, so I had no doubt another round of thunderstorms could be in our future.

The rain had caused minor flooding in low-lying areas, so I took it slow once I reached pavement as well. I turned on the radio to the easy listening station in an effort to provide a distraction from my thoughts, and to introduce a calming element to the overall atmosphere of the vehicle. I felt tense, and if I was tense, Charlie would be too, and the poor mama spaniel looked scared to death.

A few minutes later, I glanced in the rearview mirror to the seat behind me. It appeared the spaniel had gone to sleep. I didn't blame her a bit. The whole ordeal must have been very trying for a mama so far along in her pregnancy. I'd need to put Catherine in the back seat once I picked her up, so I decided to run by the house, drop off the dogs with Alex, then head over to the boathouse to pick up my baby.

******

"You found another body in Henderson House?" Ellie asked after I'd greeted Catherine, who was sitting on the floor playing with Eli. Or at least playing near him. It didn't seem as if she necessarily cared whether he was there or not. "Doesn't that make three bodies you've found in that house?"

"I didn't technically find the parapsychologist who died four years ago, so in terms of bodies I've found in the house, this only makes two. This is the third murder that's taken place in that house in the past five years, however."

"Someone should just tear that place down. The number of people who have died in that house over the years is ridiculous. I'm not one to be superstitious, but I'd almost be willing to bet the place is cursed. Do you know who this victim is?"

I shook my head, lifting my lips on one side in a sort of half grin. "I didn't recognize him, but I can tell you that the killer was a vampire."

Ellie lifted both brows. "A vampire?"

"The guy had these two little holes in his neck that looked exactly like a vampire bite."

"You know vampires aren't real."

I lifted one shoulder, enjoying the look of disbelief on Ellie's face. "Maybe."

She began to catch onto my game and rolled her eyes. "Why would someone make a murder look like a vampire attack? It feels weird and intentional."

"It *was* weird and intentional." I went on to explain my theory that the killer had specifically intended for me to be the one who found the body. I shared my thoughts about the dog being tied in the basement and the call to the Zoo when I would be the only one there.

"So you think you were lured there?" Ellie gasped. "That terrifies me."

I bit my lower lip, a more serious mood overtaking me. "Yeah. The fact that the scene seemed to have been set for my benefit is bothering me as well."

"You don't think it was Claudia…?" Ellie asked.

Claudia Lotherman was a woman I suppose could be classified as my archnemesis. Not only had she tried to kill me twice in the last several years but she'd kidnapped Zak the previous spring and made me pass a bunch of tests to get him back. The last I heard, she was still in the wind and no one knew exactly where she'd holed up, but I had a hard time believing she'd come back to Ashton Falls when so many people were looking for her. Still, she *had* concocted an elaborate scheme when she kidnapped Zak.

"I suppose it's possible Claudia is behind this," I agreed. "The vampire thing seems like something she'd do, and she's a master of disguise, so she might be able to slip into town unnoticed. But it seems like a huge risk for her to come back here so soon after her last visit, so I'm thinking it isn't her, even if she is a total loon. So, maybe. I'll mention it to Salinger when he calls later and see what he thinks."

"If the person who killed that man and left him for you to find wasn't Claudia, then who?" Ellie asked.

"With everything you've told me it really does sound like you're being targeted. Someone really seems to want to mess with you. We know Claudia will go to great lengths just to yank your chain, but other than her, I can't think of a single person who would go to so much trouble. I mean really, a vampire? Who would do such a thing?"

I wished I knew. The idea that someone had set up the murder for my benefit bothered me quite a lot. I had to wonder if the body I'd found in the basement was the beginning and the end to whatever was going to happen, or if there were other people at risk of being killed just so someone could get at me. I'd been struggling with that idea ever since I'd found the body, that perhaps I was the reason a man had died on this blustery day in late October. I just couldn't figure out how anyone could possibly know the details of that first death all those years ago.

"Do you need me to watch Catherine tomorrow?" Ellie asked when I didn't speak for a couple of minutes.

"No," I answered, pulling myself out of my thoughts and into the present. "I plan to be home. Do you want to come over? We can work on a menu for the Halloween Spooktacular. I'd like to do theme foods, the way we have in the past, and of course we'll need chicken wings for Levi. But I thought we could add some new things as well. Maybe we can throw in a few more desserts. I bought a Halloween recipe book when I went to the market last week. I bet we can find some ideas in it that haven't occurred to us before."

"I'd love to come by your place for a visit, and I do want to go over the menu, but I have a doctor's appointment in the morning, so it'll have to be in the afternoon."

"Is everything okay?" I asked. Ellie was pregnant with child number two.

"Everything is perfect, although I'm a little nervous. Tomorrow is the day I finally find out the sex of the baby."

I smiled. "That's great. I've been dying to know. I don't know why you waited so long to have the ultrasound."

Ellie let out a breath. "I guess I was scared, so I procrastinated."

I narrowed my gaze. "Scared? Why? Because you're hoping for a girl and will be disappointed if it's a boy, or do you want another boy and will be let down if it's a girl?"

"Exactly."

"To which one?" I asked.

"Both."

Books by Kathi Daley

Come for the murder, stay for the romance.

Zoe Donovan Cozy Mystery:
Halloween Hijinks
The Trouble With Turkeys
Christmas Crazy
Cupid's Curse
Big Bunny Bump-off
Beach Blanket Barbie
Maui Madness
Derby Divas
Haunted Hamlet
Turkeys, Tuxes, and Tabbies
Christmas Cozy
Alaskan Alliance
Matrimony Meltdown
Soul Surrender
Heavenly Honeymoon
Hopscotch Homicide
Ghostly Graveyard
Santa Sleuth
Shamrock Shenanigans
Kitten Kaboodle
Costume Catastrophe
Candy Cane Caper
Holiday Hangover
Easter Escapade
Camp Carter
Trick or Treason
Reindeer Roundup
Hippity Hoppity Homicide

Firework Fiasco
Henderson House – *August 2018*

Zimmerman Academy The New Normal
Ashton Falls Cozy Cookbook

Tj Jensen Paradise Lake Mysteries by Henery Press:

Pumpkins in Paradise
Snowmen in Paradise
Bikinis in Paradise
Christmas in Paradise
Puppies in Paradise
Halloween in Paradise
Treasure in Paradise
Fireworks in Paradise
Beaches in Paradise

Whales and Tails Cozy Mystery:

Romeow and Juliet
The Mad Catter
Grimm's Furry Tail
Much Ado About Felines
Legend of Tabby Hollow
Cat of Christmas Past
A Tale of Two Tabbies
The Great Catsby
Count Catula
The Cat of Christmas Present
A Winter's Tail
The Taming of the Tabby
Frankencat

The Cat of Christmas Future
Farewell to Felines
A Whisker in Time – *September 2018*
The Catsgiving Feast – *November 2018*

Writers' Retreat Mystery:
First Case
Second Look
Third Strike
Fourth Victim
Fifth Night
Sixth Cabin
Seventh Chapter

Rescue Alaska Paranormal Mystery:
Finding Justice
Finding Answers
Finding Courage - *September 2018*
Finding Christmas – *November 2018*

A Tess and Tilly Mystery:
The Christmas Letter
The Valentine Mystery
The Mother's Day Mishap
The Halloween House
The Thanksgiving Trip – *October 2018*

Haunting by the Sea:
Homecoming by the Sea
Secrets by the Sea
Missing by the Sea – *October 2018*

Sand and Sea Hawaiian Mystery:

Murder at Dolphin Bay
Murder at Sunrise Beach
Murder at the Witching Hour
Murder at Christmas
Murder at Turtle Cove
Murder at Water's Edge
Murder at Midnight

Seacliff High Mystery:

The Secret
The Curse
The Relic
The Conspiracy
The Grudge
The Shadow
The Haunting

Road to Christmas Romance:

Road to Christmas Past

USA Today best-selling author Kathi Daley lives in beautiful Lake Tahoe with her husband Ken. When she isn't writing, she likes spending time hiking the miles of desolate trails surrounding her home. She has authored more than seventy-five books in eight series, including Zoe Donovan Cozy Mysteries, Whales and Tails Island Mysteries, Sand and Sea Hawaiian Mysteries, Tj Jensen Paradise Lake Series, Writers' Retreat Southern Seashore Mysteries, Rescue Alaska Paranormal Mysteries, and Seacliff High Teen Mysteries. Find out more about her books at **www.kathidaley.com**

Stay up-to-date:
Newsletter, *The Daley Weekly* – **http://eepurl.com/NRPDf**
Webpage – **www.kathidaley.com**
Facebook at Kathi Daley Books –
www.facebook.com/kathidaleybooks
Kathi Daley Books Group Page –
https://www.facebook.com/groups/569578823146850/
E-mail – **kathidaley@kathidaley.com**
Twitter at Kathi Daley@kathidaley
https://twitter.com/kathidaley
Amazon Author Page –
https://www.amazon.com/author/kathidaley
BookBub – **https://www.bookbub.com/authors/kathi-daley**

AUG 1 5 2018

PP Rot 2/19

ROT GT 6/19

TR MN 1/20

SLT

22116372R00104

Made in the USA
Columbia, SC
28 July 2018